AF493280

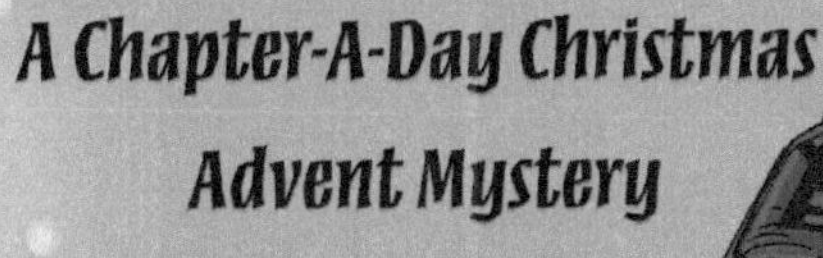

Originally Published in
April 2026

* * *

A Standalone Novella

* * *

Written and Illustrated
by Sarah Ickes

Cozy Mystery | Historical | Whimsical

"You know I'm more careful than a walrus."

Thank you...

to my Beta Readers, Sherry and Sherry, for taking time out of their busy schedules to help me make this book into the best it can be!

A Special Note for You...
Dear Reader.

This mystery is meant to be read one chapter a day for twelve days, as an advent. But that does not mean you have to abide by such rules.

If you would prefer to sit and binge through the chapters instead, that is entirely your decision.

So have fun with this story, and read it any way you wish. Because you are in for a fantastical ride.

Merry Christmas!

- Sarah (a fellow reader)

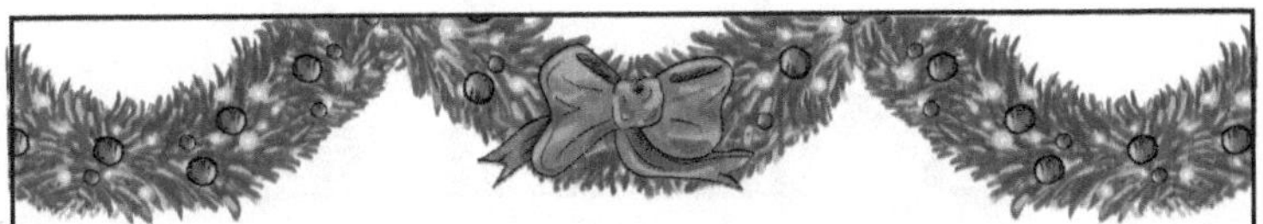

<u>Your Twelve Days of Advent</u>

Characters

Bobby Joe "BJ" Coppersmith
(Yuletown's Sheriff)

Beauregard "Beau"
(Bobby Joe's Golden Retriever Mix)

Archie Becker
(Deputy Sheriff)

Eric Newsome
(Deputy Sheriff)

Adriana and Liza Coppersmith
(Bobby Joe's Young Twin Cousins)

Eve Coppersmith
(Bobby Joe's Mother)

Norma Jean Coppersmith
(Bobby Joe's Sister)

Montgomery "Mont" Sr.
(Town Hall Worker)

<u>The Wagner's Bakery:</u>

Molly Wagner........................... Steven and Angus's Sister

Angus Wagner........................... Steven and Molly's Brother

Steven Wagner........................... Angus and Molly's Brother

Reggie Wagner........................... Steven's Son

Grace Wagner........................... Steven's Daughter

Characters

Other Townsfolk:

Edwina Payton.......................... Timmy's Sister

Timmy Payton.......................... Edwina's Brother

Vance Krogger.......................... Timmy's Friend

Hans Schmidt.......................... Archie's Friend

Ferdinand Schmidt................. Hans's Son

Mrs. Healy............................... Bookshop Owner

Mrs. Anthony............................ Cookie Contest Judge

Among others who will be revealed in due time...

Chapter 1

On the First Day of Christmas

Bobby Joe Coppersmith gazed out at the scene sprawled before him. The town was alive with a new-found energy he hadn't witnessed in such a long time; as the feeling of the holiday season seemed to consume the entire population of Yuletown. Even the old beggar had removed himself from the front steps of Mr. Montgomery's store without being asked…and that was a miracle in itself.

Lanterns lined the streets in all directions, lit with the same warming glow they were every night. But on the eve of December first, it suddenly felt different. The Christmas wreaths were securely attached to the black metal poles in a way that would survive a small tornado. While that wasn't much of a problem where they lived, it was the pride and joy of Mr. Montgomery's father to do the best job he knew how. He believed that if you couldn't step away from your work with a smile at what you had accomplished, then you were required to do it until it was right. Hard work had been their family's mantra for as long as any of them could remember; which included ancestral notes in an old leather-bound bible from 1795.

Watching the patriarch of the family stepping down

from a well-used ladder, Bobby Joe walked up to greet the man who'd taught him how to fish as a young boy. Since his own father had vanished when he was nearly seven years old, the eldest Montgomery was the closest thing to a father figure he had. That was what made the news much more difficult to deliver; for if it had been anyone else, other than Montgomery Senior, he wouldn't have felt so torn up inside.

"Tell me, B.J., what do you think?" The wrinkles on the seventy-year-old man's face disappeared when the grin formed on his lips, gazing up at the wreath with a fresh bow he'd made that afternoon. "I changed the ragged red bows to a darker cranberry color this year. Time for a change, I so felt." His long whiskers shook slightly from chuckling as he snapped the ladder together and prepped the next set of greenery.

"They look great, Mont." While Bobby Joe was known by most as B.J., he was the only person who was allowed to call Montgomery Senior by his childhood nickname. Before the epic battle of the Montgomerys ten years ago, in the middle of the town square no less, Junior would some-times use that name when he needed his father's immediate attention. However, their extremely public fight outside the shop ended that relationship in a fiery demise. Sometimes B.J. even swore he could still hear their harsh words slicing through what had been an otherwise peaceful afternoon that July. And his friendship with Junior hadn't been the same since.

"I think I might have broken my record from last year." Mont's eyes dazzled like a clear night sky as he checked his pocket watch. He clicked his black boot heels like a giddy school boy and tapped his finger on the right side of his nose. "Did thirty an hour instead of twenty-six!"

"Mont, you shouldn't be pushing yourself so much!" B.J.

swiftly moved his hand to his jacket's right pocket, where the dooming decision was stowed inside. "You could hurt yourself keeping that pace."

A simple wave in the cold air told the town's sheriff what Mont really thought of his concern. "Fiddlesticks! I've never felt better and what's life without a little challenge? Eh?"

"Funny you should mention that…" As B.J. unearthed the folded piece of paper with his shaky fingers, anxiety began to build in his throat. He feared what this might do to the man he respected for most of his life, and despised having to be the one to enforce it. "Mont, I…"

"Hey, where is that dog of yours?" The older man swung his head around to scan the sidewalks in search of B.J.'s usual companion. He half-expected to see a mound of golden fur jogging past one of the local businesses or sniffing a piece of litter near the side of the road. But Beauregard was nowhere in sight. "It isn't like Beau to not be by your side."

B.J. instantly shot a worrisome glance to his left, where his golden retriever mix would normally be waiting with a wagging tail and a friendly smile. Sure enough, his best friend was gone and a torn newspaper blew by his leg as the wind picked up. "That's odd, he was just there a minute ago."

Rapidly shoving the paper into his pocket once again, B.J. retraced his steps to the grocery store where he had recently purchased some ingredients for a holiday recipe. There was no sign of his dog by the truck nor at the entrance to Mr. Montgomery's store. *Now I know that Beau was with me when we loaded the food onto the back seat. And he could not have rushed by me without me seeing him. Could he have? B.J. had been preoccupied most of the day, so it might have been possible that Beau walked off without him knowing it. One thing is for sure, though. After I find him, he is going back on the leash!*

"There!" Mont called out, pointing his bony finger toward an alleyway where construction had been going on for over a year. "I saw the tip of his tail as he headed toward the dead end."

B.J. cautiously approached the alley with his eyes on alert for anything suspicious. If Beau traveled that far away without him, it was not a good sign. Ever since he was a puppy, Beau had a knack of sniffing out trouble and it didn't take his owner long to realize that he was born to be a detective in his own right. Still, whenever he didn't bark to tell B.J. something was amiss, there was a good reason for it. *Why could it not have been a squirrel or a little bird that was injured? But nope. He HAD to head down the creepy alley that practically dead ends in three blocks.*

"Beau?" The sheriff's voice was unsteady at best, as he resisted the urge to shout for his dog. "Where are you?"

Silence was all that met his ears as he glanced around overflowing trash bins and scattered cardboard boxes that dotted the alley. The tall brick buildings surrounded the darkening passage with a suffocating appearance, causing the entire area to feel foreign and unwelcoming. Forcing his feet to press on down a narrow path, B.J. continued to head deeper into the eerie construction section of town. With each step he took, however, he couldn't help but feel as though someone was watching him. "Beau?"

B.J.'s heart nearly stopped when he suddenly heard barking coming from around the bend to his left. Sprinting past the corner, the sheriff soon found himself watching his dog going crazy over a pair of empty shoes sitting in the middle of a group of small stones. A swirling cloud of dust was just beginning to settle upon the churned up landscape, and the faint smell of perfume was fading from the scene. Determined to tell his owner all that he knew, Beau kept barking while shifting his attention between the shoes and B.J.'s shocked face.

No. It can't be.

Chapter 2

Those Are No Elf Shoes

Mont hobbled up behind B.J. and peered around the sheriff's taller frame to see what all of the excitement was about. His eyebrows squinched together when he saw the empty shoes standing upright in the middle of the desolate alley. From what he could tell, they were ordinary brown boots, whose laces were new and still knotted as though they were attached to a ghostly being. But when he moved in closer, against B.J.'s orders, Mont's head moved back in surprise. "Those belong to Molly Wagner. See the scuff marks on the front?" Pointing to where the marks were located on the shoes' rounded toe area, Mont made sure not to touch the evidence with his own fingers. "She just got those all marked up while tripping over my boxes of wreaths."

"Do you know precisely how long ago?"

"Could not have been more than ten minutes, the way I reckon. She had been walking homebound from the Community Center, and you know how much of a stickler Mrs. Anthony is for closing the doors exactly at seven p.m. sharp!" Mont reached down to pet Beau on the top of his head, ensuring that he scratched behind the dog's itchy ears.

"That must have been right before you parked your truck by the store."

B.J. didn't know what to make of it. Molly was a woman in her late thirties who was used to walking over five miles a day and helped her family deliver baked goodies on a regular basis. In essence, she wasn't a thin twig of a woman and knew how to handle herself. *She didn't scream out a call for help. I wonder why?* He cast a puzzling look at his dog, wishing Beau could plainly tell him what he saw or noticed that made him travel down this way. Not many of the townspeople ventured toward the new construction sites as the future buildings were being put in place; and for good reason. If it wasn't creepy enough during the day, with no workers anyone could see, the entire lots took on a haunted house feeling as soon as evening fell.

Despite the fact that building during the holiday season seemed very odd to the people of Yuletown, they had grown accustomed to the unique habit over the years. But it was the whispering of noises at night that had them racing home as soon as possible from work, and the occasional spotlights that would stir their imaginations. With the strange way that the new structures would suddenly appear completed and ready to use, some of the residents believed the workers to be Christmas elves who wielded the power of invisibility. Others were of the opinion that they were the ghosts of past mine workers still paying off their debt for setting fire to the town in 1864. Regardless of the fantastical explanations many of the sheriff's neighbors had created, B.J. wasn't one for blaming the supernatural before ruling out all logical reasoning. *Although my mother would highly disagree with me.*

Mont's lower lip quivered in dread. "Do you think it could be the…"

"No, I do not." B.J. abruptly cut down the elder Montgomery's question. He had no time to entertain the notion that the town's "Beast" had returned after all this time. If their local newspaper, *The Harking Herald*, was to print a headline to that effect, the town would be in an uproar and pressure from the council would rest squarely on his shoulders. It was bad enough he hadn't delivered the message to Mont as of yet, without adding another thing for them to complain about.

"Even now, twenty-seven years later, you still deny it to be true? Why? 'The Beast' is real, B.J. That much I know." Mont may never have stepped foot into an ocean, but B.J. swore he was ready to believe any fisherman's tale told to him. It was the one thing the two of them had argued about off and on for the last five years. Regardless of the fact that no new evidence was ever brought forth, the older man felt that it was time Bobby Joe accept what happened to his father was not of this world.

"We have been over this before, Mont. The idea that a phantom being would steal people in the middle of the night is simply insane. And I refuse to believe that Krampus made the journey over here from the 'Old Country' because our town is cursed! Let alone the fact that if there is any connection…though slim that may be…over two decades is a long time between incidents." B.J. glanced about the darkened area, searching in vain for some kind of a clue as to what really had happened. In the dimly lit space, however, the only thing out of place was the three of them standing around the pair of shoes.

Since most of the town's families hailed from Germany, often referred to as the "Old Country" by the elder generations, some of them thought there to be a curse upon their town from abandoning their ancestral homelands. To seek vengeance, Krampus followed them to America and waited until they were prospering in order to steal their kin. Again, another tale B.J. was above believing. *There has to be a simple answer...*

Beau barked at his owner and wagged his tail with a serious expression on his muzzle. While Molly Wagner's disappearance was very similar to those in the past, this was his chance to prove to everyone that it was not the doing of some mythical beast. This time, he was the one who was going to solve the case and find her before Christmas arrived! *First, we need to establish that it was really Molly who went missing. Then I will have to contact her brothers at the bakery.*

Turning to the witness, B.J. started asking Mont some questions; such as did Molly appear out of sorts when he saw her last, was she carrying anything suspicious with her, and was there anyone following her as she walked past him? Although Mont didn't have all the answers to the sheriff's inquiries, he did his best, and kept returning back to the moment she ran into his boxes of wreaths. "It was odd. Rather odd, I tell ya."

"Can you explain?"

"Well, while she didn't seem to be acting out of the usual, I found it weird that she tripped into my boxes at all. I had pointed out to her where they were, and she nodded to me that she saw them. And still, she managed to step right into them. It was like…" Mont scratched his drying chin in the colder weather, "like she had clumsy feet, or the shoes weren't hers to begin with." His eyes suddenly widened as it dawned on him. "Say, come to think of it, I bet those shoes are a few sizes too large for her feet."

"That would back up the fact that they are standing upright as though she slipped out of them without a trace."

B.J. instructed both Mont and Beau to stand guard as he headed back to his truck to radio for one of his deputies. He hated the idea of leaving them both near the eerie construction lots so late in the evening, but he wanted some help in surveying the area before removing the boots as evidence. After all, perhaps Molly was still nearby and the case would be over that night.

It took a few minutes to get ahold of Deputy Archie Becker, who had apparently fallen asleep to some Christmas music coming from his Victrola. But the fifty-seven-year-old man pinched himself wide awake when he heard that Molly might be missing. He had been her second grade teacher once upon a blue moon, and he always had a soft spot for the student that loved music history. "Be there as fast as I can, Sheriff."

"Bring two extra flashlights, you hear?"

"Right."

Not twenty minutes later, Archie could be seen coming down in the station's only vehicle. It was an older Mercury 8 Patrol car that was in desperate need of a good wash and a set of new tires. B.J. felt that it was better for him to use his father's 1935 Chevy Master Canopy Truck so that the other guys had something to get around in while on duty.

"Good timing, Archie." B.J. waited for him to park along the road, and then directed him to where the shoes were still standing between Beau and Mont.

"Just like her Pa, ain't it?" Archie had goosebumps crawling up his skin from the déjà-vu of the scene. "And like your's as well, B.J."

"That's what I have been saying!" Mont exclaimed just as the sheriff was about to deny the claim. "But he doesn't think that 'The Beast' has returned."

"I did not invite Archie here for a cultural debate on

the unexplained. Alright?!" B.J.'s patience was growing thin between the both of them. "Look, we are going to do a search of the area to see if Molly is anywhere to be found, or if there are any other clues to her whereabouts. Then I will go to have a chat with her brothers. Is that clear?"

"Sure thing, Boss." Archie straightened his back and rested his hand atop the pistol at his side. "But weren't you getting some groceries for your mother?"

B.J.'s cheeks flushed with embarrassment. He had completely forgotten about the food in his back seat, and there was a gallon of milk waiting to be taken home. "Like I said, I will be talking with the Wagner brothers after stopping off at my mother's house. Now let's get to work."

As Mont took the sections to the west, Archie picked the northern end, which left the easterly lots for B.J. to tend to with Beau. Gulping down his fear, the sheriff instructed his dog to stay by his side and bravely stepped into the darkened construction. He pulled the collar of his jacket closer toward his neck as the wind swept through the canvas-covered scaffolding. The moist feeling of snow could be felt in the air, which was going to make all of the kids very happy in the morning.

Clicking the flashlight on, the small beam of light did little to penetrate into the abyss. "Molly? Are you here?" B.J.'s soft voice sounded distant in the vast realm of the new layout being developed. This was to be one of the largest expansions ever added to their town. Apparently the new projects were top secret, as they always were, so no one quite knew what was coming; a point that unsettled the business owners until the grand unveilings. "Molly Wagner? Where are you?" He could hear the sound of metal scraping against brick as his foot bumped into a large building tool. It was something he swore looked familiar, but was on a scale he had never seen before. *Oh great! If I tell anyone about this, they are going to think BigFoot is helping the elves to build our town.*

Beau bumped into B.J.'s leg near the start to a newly paved road that was curving into the forest. Staring into the blackened wall of fir and maple trees, the air was quieter than a monastery and seemed determined to keep its secrets. It was soon becoming clear to the sheriff that they were not going to get any answers that night, so after a few more moments of pure anxiety, B.J. headed back with a watchful eye over his shoulder. *Just like my father.* Archie's voice sounded in his mind as an owl hooted in the trees. *My father ran off to the other side of the mountain. That's what he did.*

Looking at it today, no one would have believed that their current City Hall and Community Park had once been just as spooky and bone-chilling a sight as this one now was. But it had been just as desolate a place while being built twenty-seven years ago. B.J. was almost seven when his father had disappeared near the construction zone, and was never heard from again. That year, the so-called "Beast" had claimed twelve lives, prompting the town to enforce a curfew at five p.m. B.J. still remembered being told by then Sheriff Bell, about his father's shoes being the only thing left behind. The officers had done everything in their power to locate the missing souls, but the case remained unsolved in the file cabinet.

"There you are!" Mont was obviously relieved to see B.J. walking back to where the shoes were still waiting. "Was wondering if you'd make it out alive." He took his hand and playfully punched the sheriff in the arm with deceptive strength.

"Ow!" B.J. winced. "Are you helping out at the railyard

in your spare time still?"

"Yep! They need the help more so than ever this year. Since the cost of sending packages has actually decreased, the incoming mail has doubled."

"Did you find anything?" Archie asked. His clean face had now been dirtied by soot, his clothes had remnants of half-eaten trash hanging from a few threads, and his shoes needed a good shining from the dirt caked onto their surface.

"No. What happened to you? Did you go searching in the trash cans?"

"Oh, this." The deputy rolled his eyes. "The cat won. There is nothing more I wish to say on the matter."

Mont couldn't help but chuckle, causing his pale cheeks to shine in the low light. "Mrs. Anthony's feline had him cornered."

"Enough, Old Timer." Archie raised an eyebrow at Mont. "That tabby has never liked me from the start."

B.J. merely shook his head as he reached down to get a better look at the shoes with his flashlight. "We better have these boots marked into evidence and open a case file on Molly. Archie, can you handle it?" He looked up at the deputy who stunk worse than a skunk.

"Sure thing, B.J." Archie stooped to the ground and picked them up by their tied laces, wondering if there might be some truth in the lore of their construction workers. "What do you think happened, Boss?"

"I honestly haven't the slightest idea right now." B.J. admitted aloud. "But we are going to get to the bottom of this. That, you can count on!"

Chapter 3

The Recipe Calls For Milk and Vanilla

Unlike other towns, Yuletown was a time capsule in itself. The entire population lived as though it was still the 1950s and that was the way they liked it. Most of the vehicles on the roads were made before 1945, newspaper boys threw rolled-up papers at the doors every week, and more people had radios in their homes than television sets. Porch lights were welcoming glows on the townhouses down the smaller streets, where kids played on the sidewalks with their friends. Quaint yards were used for both grass and gardening whenever it wasn't below freezing outside; and the best lemonade stands were always hosted near the Müller's house on Apple Avenue. Yes, living in Yuletown was a world not only moving at a slower pace, but it was the type of area you would find on the front of a picturesque greeting card.

Although, I doubt anyone would buy a card with a missing person featured in a Rockwell painting. B.J. pulled to a stop and turned his truck onto Mulberry, where he parked it in front of a Victorian-styled two-story house. The shutters needed replacing, the molding was slightly cracked under the porch roof, and the steps were a little creaky whenever weight was applied. Regardless of the building's faults, however, it had been his home ever since he was born.

Beau looked happily through the window at the house, and then reached over from the passenger seat to nudge his muzzle under B.J.'s right arm. His eyes gazed up at his owner, wondering when he was going to open the door so they could go inside. As his nose hit against one of B.J.'s pockets, the sound of crinkling paper was a nasty reminder of what he hadn't done.

"The worst part of my job." B.J. reached down and unfolded the order from the town council that he had been directed to serve Mont a week ago. The coldly written words were like a serrated knife blade. Since Montgomery Jr.'s friend had been voted onto a seat this past election, it had been decided that the wreaths were to be hung by a younger person with a lower pay the following year. This was to be the older man's last time as the wreath hanger. "How am I going to tell him, Beau?"

The golden retriever mix raised his head upon hearing his name.

"I mean, that job is everything to him. He looks forward to doing the wreaths every year, and even has a countdown calendar to when the first of December comes. He loves chatting with the folks as they walk by his ladder and injecting some Christmas spirit into the town. Especially after the year we have been having." B.J.'s sigh was visible in the cold vehicle, prompting him to jump out and grab the groceries from the back seat as Beau struggled to wait patiently until he opened the other door. "We're going to help Mont, Beau. Somehow, we are going to find a way to make it right…after we locate Molly Wagner."

A single bark from his furry companion was both a response in agreement and an alert to those inside the house that they were home. B.J. couldn't help but stare at the yellow-orange glow of a taper candle in the window, the beautiful greenery adorning the railing, and the smell of fresh cinnamon sticks decorating the front wreath. It all looked the same each Christmas, and it just wouldn't feel right if the small angel didn't silently sing her song next to the candle. His hand was about to knock on the door just as his ears picked up on some shushing coming from inside. A smile formed on his lips when his twin cousins threw the door open for him and he saw the state of their appearances. "I can see you two have been having fun baking today."

Both girls giggled in glee at the sight of Beau, allowing for small bits of flour to fall from their cheeks. "You should see the kitchen," chuckled the one called Adriana, while her sister, Liza, licked some dough from her own teeth. Besides their hair colors being different, their facial features were almost identical, and their energy levels were not to be matched by the other ten-year-olds in town.

"Not sure I want too." B.J. watched Beau leave him on the porch as the girls fawned over him, and shook his head at the shameless way his dog abandoned him for the attention. "I thought you were man's best friend!" He joked, before turning his next question back to his cousins. "So, which recipe are you making?"

"Which one haven't we made!" They laughed again in near perfect unison.

Liza was the first to stop petting Beau and reached for the bag in B.J.'s hands. "Did you get what we asked for?"

He quickly pulled the ingredients out of arm's length. "Whoa there. What do you say? I haven't even entered the house yet." B.J. gestured to the porch where he was still standing.

"May we *please* have the milk and vanilla?" The girl's

eyes pleaded in the cutest way imaginable, knowing full well that her cousin caved in whenever she did; at least most of the time, that is. Her sister clapped her hands happily when he gave the bag over and they both hastily thanked him as they ran into the kitchen. Their feet sounded like a stampede against the wooden floorboards, causing an older woman's voice to call out from behind the door.

"What did I tell you two? Hmm? No running in the kitchen! How many times do I have to remind you two of that?!" A greying brunette leaned forward with a commanding hand that stopped the twins dead in their tracks. "I have the stove piping hot…and if one of you gets yourselves burned, why…the cake wouldn't be the only thing that ends up baked!"

"Yes, Great Aunt Eve." Liza and Adriana gently placed the bag of food on the counter and went over to the wash basin to clean some of the dishes in silence.

Upon hearing the front door finally being shut, the older woman glanced over her rounded glasses to see her son now standing in the living room. His hands were stuffed in his pockets like usual and Beau was lying down beside the warm fireplace, where his golden fur became more vibrant in the light from the flickering flames. Even though B.J. was fully grown in everyone else's eyes, all Eve Coppersmith saw was her seven-year-old boy awkwardly looking around at the remnants of his life. It was at this time of the year especially, that her heart felt the pain of her husband's disappearance all over again. "I thought you were lost or something had happened to that truck of yours! What took you so long at the store? And did you go to the barber like I asked you to?"

B.J. combed his somewhat messy hair with his hand like a child who had been scolded. "No, Mother. Not yet. After purchasing the groceries…"

"Floyd is not getting any younger, you know. His cuts are going to be shaky by the time you walk into his shop." Eve glared up at her son, who was almost a foot taller than the top of the bun on her head. Her squinting eyes studied his untrimmed locks with a disapproving look on her face. "And what is your sister to think when she arrives day after tomorrow?"

"I…"

His mother cut him off mercilessly. "I realize you secretly hope that she isn't coming home for Christmas, given your differences and all, but she truly is coming back this year, Bobby. Whether you like it or not, she is returning to Yuletown for Christmas."

"It is just that…" B.J.'s face hung low as he looked at the wood grain between his feet, "I don't wish for you to get hurt when she doesn't show up…again."

Eve placed a caring hand against his left cheek, speaking directly to him as though no one else existed in the house. "But she will this year, Bobby. I can feel it." She gave her son a wink before returning to the troublesome twins in the kitchen. Her fingers swept some curly strands away from her eyes as she adjusted the apron keeping her clothes clean of all batter. "Alright, Adriana and Liza, that is enough washing for the moment. Now, I need you to pour out these measurements for the liquid parts and I'll take care of the dry. Be careful not to spill anything on the counter."

"Mother?" B.J. stuck his head into the forbidden room, hoping to catch her attention before she became waist deep in the recipe and ignored him completely. "I need to speak to you about something important." When it came to gossip in the town, his mother had a talent for being close to the heartbeat of the rumor mill.

Noticing the serious notes in his voice, Eve decided it was best for the girls to make old-fashioned ornaments for the Christmas tree in another room. She hurriedly grabbed four oranges, along with a pile of cloves, and led the girls out of the kitchen. No more than fifteen seconds later, she had rejoined B.J. waiting near the mixer, and shut the doors for privacy. "Come out with it then. We have a few good minutes until they are finished with their fruits."

Not knowing how his mother was going to react to the news, B.J. tried to ease his way into the conversation. "Okay, something happened tonight that I need to ask your help on. I am not sure…well, let us just…just…"

Eve's eyes widened in fear, and her white cheeks turned a shade of pink. "There has not been more disappearances, has there?!"

B.J. merely blinked. There was no possible way for his mother to have already learned about the incident. Then again, she always did have a knack for knowing about the bad news before he was going to say it; and she would often deny having heard it from anyone else prior to their discussions. "Actually, Molly Wagner has vanished, according to Mont…who identified her as being the one who was in the shoes left behind. But how did you find out? Mont went back to his wreath when I left to come here, and I have Archie taking them to the station for evidence."

"Oh no." Eve's right hand flew to her mouth in concern. "We have to warn Edwina. I was so wrong…so very wrong."

Chapter 4

The Christmas Tree Will Have to Wait

"What do you mean 'you were wrong?'" B.J. had an awful feeling growing in the pit of his stomach. Whenever his mother had that look on her face, it always meant something bad was happening, or was about to.

"Edwina called earlier this evening, asking for you. She actually called the station first, and was told that you were on your way here by Archie. He offered to help her, but you know how she is on 'only speaking to the sheriff.'"

Unless she wants to gossip with you, Mother. B.J. reached up to rub his left eyebrow, not wanting to hear another episode from the Payton family saga. Those two siblings were as thick as thieves, and Edwina's brother was often thirstier than a fish in a desert whenever the cold air settled in town. His drinking habits consisted more of whiskey over the other varieties, which is why The Spice Man made sure to be fully stocked around the holidays. "Let me guess, it has something to do with Timmy?"

His mother solemnly nodded as she reached for the back of her neck. "She said his bed was unslept in last night, and she was terribly worried that something had happened to him. I told her that he was probably sleeping it off at the bar. And then she said they saw him leave around closing time and haven't heard from him since."

B.J. glanced down to check the time on his worn wristwatch. Despite there being a few scratches in the otherwise smooth glass surface, he could still read that it was already eight-thirty in the evening. *The Spice Man opens at four, and his shift at the hotel ends at six, so Timmy would have been there by now.* "I'll have Archie pay Vance Krogger a visit. He is probably over there with a bad hangover as we speak." He shook his head. "Ol' Jerry is not going to be as easy to convince to keep him on the payroll after this one. I mean…"

"Vance is away at his brother's house on the other side of the mountain," his mother hastily interrupted, "and he took back the key he gave Timmy after his last unexpected visit." Eve motioned to the stove in a simple gesture, referring to the past April when Timmy nearly caught his friend's house on fire by leaving the heating element on. "It's clear to me that something else could have happened."

"Okay…I'll have Archie check out the house just in case. If he is not there, then I will go looking for him myself." Although this should have pleased his mother, in B.J.'s opinion, Eve's face displayed her frustrations with her son.

"Bobby Joe Augustine! How can you not see that he has most likely been taken by 'The Beast?!'"

Hearing his middle name being spoken aloud still made him cringe after all these years. "The singular fact that Timmy has not returned home is not evidence that he has vanished. He could simply be sleeping it off in Vance's yard or have passed out in an alley somewhere. I will get ahold of Archie and see if we can locate him tonight. Alright? You can call Edwina back and tell her that we are looking into the matter."

"What happened to Molly?" His mother eyed him suspiciously, waiting for an answer that he could not wriggle himself out of supplying.

B.J. sighed, and then told her what Mont said about Molly tripping over the boxes, Beau finding the shoes near the new construction site, and finished off with Archie taking the shoes back as evidence. "I have to head on over to the bakery to ask some questions. Perhaps her brothers can shine some light on this and we will find her tonight." At the end of his retelling, his mother's blank expression was unmistakable. "What?"

"I knew it. For years…*and years*…I have said that 'The Beast' would return one day!" Eve's hand slapped against the counter. "He has come back, Bobby. The shoes being left behind is proof enough of that. Not to mention that her father was one of the original…"

"The original twelve victims. I do remember that, Mother. Much like the day when Sheriff Bell sat us down in the living room to tell us the same news I must deliver to the Wagners." B.J. stared at the ground in an attempt to keep his mother from seeing his face. Even he could not have denied the uncanny similarities to the old case. No one ever saw 'The Beast' in-person, heard more than a few noises right before it happened, and each of the victims had reportedly not cried out for help. From a book writer's standpoint, it was the perfect setup for a horror novel in the making.

Eve was quiet for a moment, waiting for a heartbeat to pass in order to speak once again. "I do not envy the task ahead of you, my son. But maybe this will help in your investigation." She reached over to where a rack of cookies had been cooling from the oven.

B.J. examined the angel blowing a trumpet, decorated with white icing and a few golden sprinkles. "A cookie is going to help?"

His mother gave him a sideways glance with her eye. "It is not common knowledge that the bakery has fallen on some tough times over the past year. The Wagners have been keeping their appearances up, trying to make it seem as though their business is flourishing. But they are close to being bankrupt. So that would explain why her shoes were too large for her feet, either purchased through the second-hand store on Candle Street, or they were borrowed from one of her brothers."

"Thanks. I did not know that." B.J. bit off the angel's head and thought to himself. *If everything she said is true, then why would "The Beast" be going after their family? The last time, it only hit the wealthier crowd...except for my father.* He brushed the thought away like an annoying fly and moved toward the living room just as the door popped open to reveal the twins standing there with their spiked oranges.

"All done." Liza announced while her sister held one out for B.J. to see better.

"Want to help us put them up on the tree?" Adrianna asked hopefully.

Smiling at his cousins, B.J. regrettably had to postpone their offer. "I would love to help. Unfortunately, I have a case at work that requires my attention tonight. Perhaps tomorrow?"

"Tomorrow Great Aunt Eve promised to show us how to make fruitcake!" Liza exclaimed.

"Did she?" B.J. peered back at his mother, who was holding back a smirk. "And I am sure that your father will be delighted to hear that."

"Well, let us not dwell on the day that hasn't arrived yet." Eve motioned for the girls to put the cookies away. "I want to see a clean counter when I return."

"Bye B.J." Liza waved as she headed for the rack.

"Be safe." Adriana gave him a hug before rejoining her sister in the kitchen. There was something in the way she said it, that B.J. couldn't quite put his finger on, but he sensed that she had overheard some of their conversation.

"You know I'm more careful than a walrus." It was a saying he had invented as a child, and had clung to when he got older. He supposed it did not make much sense; although that was not the general point of it. Over the last twenty years, there was not one person who could resist the urge to chuckle at that line.

Beau felt the vibrations of his owner's feet through the floorboards and slowly blinked his eyes open from his warm haven near the fireplace. Seeing B.J. with his mother, the golden mix figured it was time to depart. Against his better wishes to stay where the rug was soft, the atmosphere was inviting, and the fire's heat pulsated gently upon his fur, Beau preferred to keep his owner in sight. There was no telling what trouble he could get into this time around.

B.J. turned to face his mother at the front door. "I'd ask for you to watch Beau while I am gone…"

"Though I doubt the neighbors would enjoy hearing him howl when he saw you were nowhere to be found after his nap." Eve gave the dog a pat on the head and touched the tip of his nose with her index finger. "Take good care of him."

"See you tomorrow." With a small kiss on her cheek, B.J. walked out to his truck with Beau in tow and helped his four-legged friend into the passenger side. It wasn't until the door to the house had closed shut, that he went over to the driver's side and noticed a folded paper lying under a branch atop the truck's hood.

B.J. picked the note up and hopped inside the vehicle. Beau sniffed the intriguing item as his owner slowly opened it, and saw the vexed look plastered on his face. The wording was plain enough, but the letters were angled slightly different, as though the writer was left-handed.

Chapter 5

Baking is a Family Tradition

The air chilled past everyone's expectations, gripping right through the skin and latching onto bones with a relentless force. Even Beau was showing signs of the cold seeping through his fur by crouching closer toward B.J. in the driver's seat. "I do believe that we will be seeing some snow here very shortly." He stroked his fingers atop his dog's head, thinking back to Timmy's unslept bed and Edwina's concerns. It had been a few minutes since he radioed Archie to check on Vance's house, and he wondered if the eldest Payton would be found sprawled out in the yard. "What do you wager, Beau?"

His furry companion blinked his eyes open.

"Will Timmy be at the house, or do we have a second disappearance on our hands?" B.J. secretly hoped that all Archie would have to do was to write up a public intoxication fine that night. Elsewise, the unimaginable had indeed returned and he was going to have two missing persons to locate. *One for each night. That is how it was. One for each night. But then again, all of the families were doing financially well last time. And if Mother is right about the Wagners, that is not the case now.*

Beau gave a quick bark to let him know that his hand had stopped petting.

"Oh my! Well I do apologize. How silly of me." As B.J. pulled up to the intersection where Orange Street crossed Cranberry Street, he paused when he saw lights inside the bakery. "How odd, Beau. One would figure that bakers should be in bed at this hour. I know that their father regimented a three a.m. start each morning when he ran the shop."

The sheriff turned to the right and parked directly across the road. From what he could see through the large bay windows, there appeared to be two younger people cleaning the counters and mopping up the floors. B.J. continued to watch for a few more minutes, trying to remember the names of those next to inherit the bakery. *If they manage to get out from under, that is.*

Beau forced his muzzle under his owner's arm, sending him pleading eyes. "I wish you could come in, Buddy. Really, I do. But I do not think their customers would enjoy finding your fur in their bread tomorrow morning." He gave the dog one more pat on the head and thought about how cold it might get in the truck while he would be breaking the bad news to Molly's family. "Give me a moment."

Stepping out of the vehicle, B.J. unearthed his emergency blanket with great ease from the back seat and wrapped his dog into a self-warming cocoon. "I promise not to be long." He flashed a smile through the frosted windows, instantly regretting not leaving him at his mother's house before journeying onto the Wagner's Bakery. There was no telling how this conversation was going to end with the temperament that Molly's brothers were known to have, and he wondered if he would be able to keep his word to Beau. *I'll use him as an excuse for me to exit stage right, if the* need should arise. That might get me out of some unwanted family drama.

B.J. just passed his one year milestone at being the town's sheriff in October; but that did not mean he hadn't conveyed terrible news to a family or two whilst he was a deputy. His predecessor warned him it did not get better with experience, and there were times when the right words seemed to fail even his mentor. Having only ten seconds to mumble and practice what he wanted to say, B.J. was disappointed to find that he was already standing at the door before he finished two sentences. His hand shakily reached for the knob, which surprisingly turned without any issues, and he gratefully walked inside the warmer building.

Since the day's final batches of bread loaves were normally pulled from the ovens around ten in the morning, most of that sweet smell of fresh dough had evaporated. The shelves were left barren and the counters were devoid of anything larger than crumbs. Baskets were empty of their delicious contents, waiting for another day's work to fill them once again. It was the sight of the red and green bows, however, that reminded the sheriff of when his father would bring him in as a boy. He would always purchase a pretzel for Young B.J. and the tantalizing scents of the bakery would allow his imagination to soar. Around this time of year, the Wagners were known for their gingerbread loaves that carried such a heavenly aroma, and even that had already escaped the kitchen.

As the two teenagers were just beginning their closing routines, having finished their homework after dinner, their attentions were so focused on sweeping the floors that they failed to notice B.J. standing by the counter.

"Ugh, Reggie, I thought you said you locked the door!" Scolded the blonde-haired girl at her brother; who was two years older in calculated time only.

"Maybe I didn't." His sheepish eyes, and shameful facial expressions, told the rest of the story. "I was in the middle of my book!" The boy attempted to stare down his sister, who was an inch taller than him, before scoffing at the air and shuffling his way back toward the mixers with his mop in tow.

"Sorry about that, Sir. My brother can be quite forgetful at times. Especially when he is reading." The girl flashed the sheriff a tired smile. "However, as you can clearly see, we are closed for the evening and will not be open until seven tomorrow morning."

Although the boy was obviously a direct descent of the Wagners, having the same strong jawline and large eyes that was a familial trait, the girl appeared to have more of her mother's features with a softer complexion and rounded cheeks. B.J. wasn't as familiar with the family's newer generation, which almost made it a little easier to tell them the reason for his visit.

"Actually, I'm not here to buy anything. I would like to speak to Steven and Angus if I can."

"My father and uncle do not like to be woken up once they're in bed." Reggie called from the back. Evidently his hearing was keen when his eyes weren't glued to the pages in his book.

"Be that as it may, I am afraid I need to speak with them as soon as possible." B.J. introduced himself and showed them his badge as proof.

Reggie shrugged his thin shoulders. "Your funeral." He chucked a wet towel into the hot water that filled the sink, and begrudgingly climbed the stairs that lead to the above living quarters.

The girl silently shifted her broom from one hand to

the other. "Is this because of last month's electric bill?" She quickly clamped her mouth shut and began with the question she should have asked first. "What is this all about?"

"You will find out soon enough. But it does not have anything to do with your unpaid bills." B.J. reassuringly dipped his head to her. "I heard you all have been dealing with a rough patch this year."

"Please don't tell anyone I mentioned it. That is a subject we don't speak of around here." She hastily went back to sweeping the floor until the harsh sound of shouting could be heard from the second floor. The girl jumped as though someone fired off a rocket next to her ear.

"That would be Steven." B.J. recognized his voice from their years in school together.

"You know my father?"

"Yeah. We go way back. It seems that his mood hasn't improved when he wakes up."

"Ain't that the truth. But he's pretty decent once he's had some coffee." B.J. took note of the girl's grin, and decided to ask her a few questions before the rest of the house was brought downstairs.

"Have things been alright between your Aunt Molly and her brothers?"

"I guess so. Haven't seen much of her since she began volunteering at the Community Center for their holiday dinners. This year, they started their meals a few weeks earlier than normal. She's back up in her room by the time I am down here to clean the shop." The girl slightly swayed from side to side, peering back toward the stairs before clearing her throat and staring directly at the sheriff. "Is my aunt alright?" The way her lips quivered at the end of her question caused B.J. to suspect there was more to the story.

"Is there something you want to tell me?"

"I had a bad feeling in my stomach when I didn't hear Aunt Molly's footsteps walking into her room tonight. She normally can be heard while I'm eating and doing my homework from school. But…"

"ALRIGHT! Who dares disturb my slumber?!" Came a gruff voice from within the shadows of the back stairs. Shortly after his booming voice filled the small space, two burly men in old nightshirts and thin robes came stomping out of the dark. "This had better be good!"

Steven, the taller of the two brothers, walked into the light ahead of Angus. Squinting his failing eyesight at the sheriff's shadowy figure, the man barely recognized his old classmate from school. "Bobby Joe, is that you?!"

"In the flesh, Steven. It's been a long time."

"Wow!" Angus, a less refined man than his brother was, scratched his dry arms and yawned into the air with the outstretched jaws of a lion. "Sheriff B.J.; now that's something I never pegged you on becoming in life. Figured you would have been a librarian or an English teacher."

"Well, all of that patience I learned while reading helps me get through the paperwork." B.J. looked to the floor for a brief second. Clearly Angus was still oblivious to town matters, and it was a logical guess that his sports addiction could have ramped up to gambling. *Perhaps that is the cause of their financial problems.*

"Get to the point, B.J. Why are you here?" Steven was never one for small talk.

"I'm looking for Molly. Is she here?"

"She's not in her room." Reggie answered as he approached from behind. "I just checked."

"What has our sister done?" Steven showed at least some genuine worry, unlike Angus's smirking mouth. "Molly didn't do anything too rash, did she? We were wondering what happened to her after dinner."

"And you didn't think to go looking for her?" B.J. wasn't quite sure what was going on here. In school, Molly's brothers were extremely protective of her and would have done anything to keep her from harm. Much to their parents' chagrin, that included a few fights the principal had to break up because one of the boys called her "ugly." It gained them a reputation for sitting in detention most of their freshman year in high school. However, no one dared to mess with their sister ever again.

"I wanted to…but…" Steven gave his brother a sideways glance.

"What happened, Bobby Joe?! Just tell us already!" Angus demanded.

"I'm afraid that she…quite frankly…disappeared this evening in the new expansion section of town. At least, we presume that the missing person is to be her." B.J. shoved one hand in his pocket, deliberately allowing the paper to crinkle inside. "Her boots were discovered standing upright in the middle of an alleyway." He paused, trying to gauge any of their reactions. But he was surprised to see that her brothers were more angry than concerned for her well-being. "There was a smell…like perfume…in the air where my dog found the boots."

"Of all the things for her to go off and do!" Angus smacked the table with a thick hand that used to shoe horses a few years back. "I would have thought she would have been more responsible than that. She promised!"

"Um," Steven placed a hand on his brother's larger shoulder to stop him from saying anything else. "There were no other clues as to where she vanished?"

"Not that I could see. However, I do plan on rechecking the area tomorrow morning to confirm this." B.J. refrained from mentioning the similarity to their father's disappearance. He was sure they had come to that conclusion on their own and didn't wish to air the obvious. *It still does not mean they are connected.*

Reggie shifted his feet uncomfortably between the two older men and wringed his hands as though their friction would warm up a fire. Out of the foursome's reactions, it was the younger ones who were expressing the most amount of concern for their aunt.

"Was everything going alright between you all? I mean, had Molly been acting strangely as of late, or do any of you know…"

"The hours are ticking away, Bobby Joe. And I think you would be spending your time more wisely by going out there and searching for our sister. There are no secrets for you to dig up here." Angus cast his brother a sharp glare that could have killed, as he turned on his heels to return up the stairs.

Best to come back and try to find out more tomorrow. I highly doubt Steven will be in a sharing mood after Angus put his foot down, the sheriff thought to himself. There was an unspoken hierarchy in the family, and one that was not based on birthright.

"Well, I have Beau in the truck and must be heading into the station to begin the case file." B.J. took a step backward from the counter as a sign he was not going to press them for answers. "If there is anything you can think of that would help me in locating your sister, please let me know." He wasn't quite sure if leaving so soon was considered to be callous or not, but given the cold feeling swirling around in the bakery, B.J. didn't think his continued presence would help the mood improve.

"Thank you for letting us know, B.J." Steven scratched

his chin and rubbed his back with opposite hands. "We do appreciate it." His eyes took on a distant look, as though he was lost in his own thoughts, as he also seemed to be retreating toward the stairs. Suddenly, he whipped around to ask the sheriff one last question. "May I have my boots back, please?"

"Sorry, Steven. I have to hold them as evidence for the moment." B.J. informed him that he would give them back after they had closed the case. He bid them all farewell for the evening, and shut the door behind himself when he left the bakery in utter silence. *What did Angus mean when he said that Molly should have been more responsible than that and that she promised? Could it be that she promised not to go near the construction area so late at night? The sheriff shook his head. No, there was more to it than that. Reggie seemed really shaken up by the news. And his sister was worried about Molly. Is there something else going on within the family? Maybe it has to do with their unpaid bills?*

Opening the door to the driver's side of the truck, B.J. immediately checked on Beau to find him happily sleeping in the warmth of the blanket. At the sound of his owner's gentle voice, the dog's eyes blinked open and he yawned while the back end of this make-shift bed moved with the force of his wagging tail. "Good boy. See, I wasn't in there long, now was I?" B.J. scratched him behind the ears and started up the vehicle. "Next stop's the station, Bud. We have a few calls to make."

Chapter 6

The Food's Getting Cold

The empty streets were both alluring and lonely as the town hall's clock chimed at the stroke of ten. While snow had yet to drop from the heavens above, the dampness in the surrounding air still signaled that it was coming. Christmas was B.J.'s favorite season of the year. Contrary to his co-workers' picks of spring and summer, the sheriff preferred bundling up in the cold rather than having to sweat it out during the hot afternoons of July and August. It was the time for drinking hot cocoa by the fireplace, reading through the long dark evenings, and listening to carols being sung outside the church. Despite his sister not having a care for the classic hot beverage, the one thing they agreed upon was the decorating of the tree. At least that was before she moved to the other side of the mountain.

B.J. sighed as he turned the wheel toward the police station while his gut churned with mixed emotions; though he wouldn't admit that to anyone if they asked. They had no actual evidence that it was Molly Wagner who went missing, nor if any person truly did disappear. *What if I am on some wild goose chase and all of this turns out to be an ill-devised prank?* The truck halted in front of the municipal building that functioned as both the police station and a place to host the town council's meetings.

The brick had been placed there nearly a century ago, at least that was what the placard said to the right side of the front entrance. A metal door hung off old hinges that previously harbored the original wooden frame it replaced three years ago. Cracks in the cement leading up to the steps contained numerous sealing patches done by one of the deputies who was bored over the summer. Considering how the sidewalk was beginning to resemble more of a quilt than an official pathway, it was going to have to be rectified come next spring.

"Hey, Boss!" Archie was walking around the corner from where the police car was to be parked. "Did you talk with the Wagners?"

"Yeah. Was not able to get far with them tonight." B.J. unlocked the door with a new key he was issued last week. "Please tell me you found Timmy in Vance's yard." He held it open until Archie and Beau were inside from the cold.

"Wish I could say I did, B.J. I looked all over town, and even asked his co-workers at the mine. Timmy is nowhere to be found." Archie placed his hat down on his desk, and picked up the needle on his record player. "Alright if we listen to a little 'White Christmas' as we get down to business?"

"I suppose." B.J. was more partial to Dean Martin's voice over Bing Crosby's, but that was an argument for another night. "Just as long as..." He stopped dead in his tracks at the sight of a strange basket resting on his chair. "What is that?!"

"Oh, Mrs. Healy had brought over your dinner at the same time you called me to meet you out at the construction site. I told her to place it on your chair and lock up when she left." Archie went over to the newly installed gas heater. "She said she packed it up with some warm cookies to keep it from getting cold on the way over here."

B.J. couldn't help but smile at the caring gift from his friend's mother. Ever since *The Andy Griffith Show* first aired, Mrs. Healy swore that she was the inspiration for Aunt Bee's character. She had been serving the police department their meals for much longer than the show had been running, and she did have the same heart-of-gold when it came to helping those in need. Mrs. Healy even ran the local bookshop after her brother and husband were killed in a mining accident years ago. With her son off to college across the mountain, B.J. had promised to stay in his friend's bedroom every couple of nights, to ensure she wasn't alone every night. The neighboring business was rehashing their original feud again, and had even dumped rotten food in front of the bookshop the previous week.

"Did you get the ingredients to your mother's for the cookies your cousins were baking?" Archie may have not been the most handsome in the mirror, but he had the brains and skills that counted in their line of work. He also happened to have a very good memory when it mattered. "I believe she was in the middle of making vanillekipferls when she called you."

"You have a remarkable knack for detail, Archie." B.J. unwrapped the food to find some fried chicken with macaroni and cheese just waiting to be devoured. "Did you have a chance to examine the boots before you went searching for Timmy?"

"A little bit. There appeared to be flour from the bakery on the bottom of the boot tread. As well as ginger spice and some dirt from the roads. Nothing out of the ordinary for shoes that would belong to the Wagners." Archie pointed to the box where he had their single piece of evidence sitting under its lid. "I wrote down everything I discovered thus far." He took a deep breath in. "Smells like you have some chicken for dinner."

"All the better to smell with, my dear." B.J. chuckled. "Are you sure you're not secretly a bloodhound?"

"Positive. Left my fleas and collar back at the shelter when I was adopted." Archie made his way past the sheriff's desk and nimbly stole a piece of chicken from the basket before B.J. could stop him. "So," he bit into the juicy meat, "what did Molly's family have to say for themselves?"

"Nothing like I was expecting." B.J. caught his deputy up on all that transpired at the bakery, and excluded the note he found on his truck from outside his mother's house. Archie had been the one to train him when he first joined the police department four years ago, and didn't wish to alarm the man who looked after him like one of the family.

"Hmmm." Archie took a moment to finish licking his fingers clean of the chicken he consumed. "You said that Reggie seemed highly disturbed by something. And that Angus was worried about a promise his sister made?"

"Yeah. It was strange, the way they were acting. As though something else was more important than the fact that their own sister has disappeared."

His deputy leaned against the smaller of the four desks arranged in a semi-circle around the room. "They're probably worried about their sister's endowment."

B.J. blinked his eyes in confusion. "Come again?"

"Well, they may call it something different nowadays, but it is essentially what it boils down to. Ferdinand, from the Schmidts, offered to pay them a wad of cash for her hand in marriage." Archie crossed his arms in front of his chest and lowered his voice to a mere whisper. "Apparently he has held a crush on her since school and when he overheard their family was hitting on tough times, he decided to use it as an opportunity."

B.J. stuffed a forkful of the macaroni and cheese into his mouth. He hadn't spoken to Ferdinand since his father, Hans, pulled him from school to be privately tutored in seventh grade. "Since when did this all happen?"

Archie rolled his eyes up at the ceiling, acting a little overdramatic, and casually placed his thumbs into the belt loops of his neatly pressed pants. "Some of us have our ears to the ground for any piece of information that might be helpful in situations just like this." He stared over at his boss and shook his head in mocked disappointment. "I thought I taught you better."

"You have me stumped." B.J. reached into the bottom right desk drawer and pulled out a dog bone for Beau to munch on atop his nearby bed. "If my mother did not know about the proposed marriage, then you did not get it from the beauty parlor gossip center."

Archie remained as silent as the grave and busied himself with the paperwork for the upcoming Annual Christkindl Market.

"So you must have learned about it from the drug store?"

"A good police officer never reveals his sources." His deputy stated in unwavering fashion, attempting to change the subject. "Did you sign off on the parking plans and the layout for the festival this year?"

Then it suddenly came to B.J.'s mind. "You played cards with your old gang again!"

"I did not!"

"You did too!" B.J. moved closer to where his deputy was now hiding his face behind the plant his mother-in-law gave him for his birthday.

"Archie…" B.J. smiled from ear to ear. "You swore to me that you would never step foot in the same room with Hans Schmidt for as long as you lived. Does that mean I am talking with a ghost?"

"I'm clearly living! Thank you very much!" The man's upper lip stiffened with his back. "But…perhaps…I did find my Friday nights to be getting a little dull after our fight."

B.J. chuckled and padded him on the shoulder. "Good. I'm glad to hear it. Now you can tell me everything else you've learned from your friends."

"That may disappoint you, B.J. Mostly we discuss things like how meat prices keep going up and how pretty the new hairdresser in town is."

"And how Hans had marked the cards to do an innocent magic trick for his six-year-old nephew, and accidently used those for your weekly game of poker?" B.J. couldn't resist the little jab at Archie.

"Regardless of what Hans says, I still think he subconsciously picked that deck up with the intent to clean me out." Archie inhaled another deep breath. "But we have moved passed that now."

B.J. decided to let the matter go and return to his food that was growing colder by the minute.

"Now, do you want me to collect together some of the old case files from the…" Archie stopped himself short of completing the sentence. He knew how his boss felt on the disappearances from before.

The sheriff didn't look up as he answered. "Might as well. Anything is possible, I guess. I have some phone calls to make anyway."

Beau cut through the silence in the room with a single bark, prompting the two men to glance out the window.

"It's begun to snow." Archie swiveled around in his chair. "Do you want me to head on out to the crime scene to put something over the area before it starts accumulating?"

"Huh?" The sheriff blinked from staring at the fluffy white world outside. "You know the rules. Technically we have to wait twenty-four hours before we can file a missing person report. Until then, no crime has been committed. I should not have even told the Wagners everything the way I did."

"And yet you did go out there to tell them. Because deep down, B. J., you know that there is something going on."

"You may be right, Archie, but if you agree with Mont… that it all connects, then there is nothing more we are going to find there. I'll have Eric station himself near the area tomorrow morning when he comes on duty." B.J. twisted the smooth handle of the magnifying glass in the palm of his hand; the same one that Archie had used to inspect the boots. "I trust Beau's judgement, and so do you, but we need to tread lightly here. If *The Harking Herald* gets a whiff of what is going on, we are going to have a full panic on our hands. Not to mention that the mayor will probably ask me if I am going to insist on a curfew, which will ruin the Christkindl Market for sure. Going out to cover a 'crime scene' for evidence is bound to raise suspicion." His mind drifted off a bit. "That also means that I shouldn't make the calls I want to until tomorrow morning either. It would definitely alert some people to the fact that something is wrong if I call now."

"Then I'll stay, just in case any other calls come in. You go home and get that dog of yours to bed."

"What's up? Your wife's family can't be staying over this far away from Christmas. Why are you volunteering to lose a night of sleep?" B.J. knew he often dozed at his desk since the evening shift was normally on the slow side. However, it was the fact that he offered to keep the midnight oil burning that piqued the sheriff's curiosity.

"Bobby, I know you. Instead of going to your mother's to get some shut-eye for the night, you are going to work on this case until your brain has strangled itself. There is nothing more you can do tonight. Go home and I will give you a call if Edwina finds Timmy, or if Molly shows up."

B.J. stopped what he was doing, as it was rare for Archie to call him by his first name. Even when he was new on their small force, the deputy had always treated him with the same respect he did with everyone else. It was one of the things that B.J. always liked about him, and part of the reason he believed his confidence grew so quickly. "I guess you're right."

"There. See? Go home and get some sleep." Archie cast him half a grin. "Besides, if we both stay up to the wee hours of the morning working, and the mayor catches us in here, he's liable to think that we're conspiring against him to take over the town for ourselves."

"Yeah." B.J. conceded with his hands in the air. "Alright, I'll go. But you have to call me if anything else changes."

"It's a deal."

B.J. called to Beau, who had to pry his eyes open at the sound of his owner's voice. "What do you say, Bud? Take a drive around the town to make one last patrol of the night? We can check in on Mrs. Healy to thank her for the meal."

A couple of barks answered that question rather quickly, and the crime-solving duo raced out to the truck through the thickening snowflakes.

Chapter 7

Does Mother Really Know Best?

Three more nights had come to pass with three additional people being reported as missing to the station. Archie and B.J. soon found themselves standing in the mayor's office with the rest of the town council looking very worried. They were also *very* adamant that the regular schedule of festivities should continue on as planned. All but one of them felt that it would provide their town with a much-needed distraction from the possible return of their notorious "Beast." However, B.J. didn't believe that it was entirely their decision to make.

"We should call an emergency meeting in the town hall and ask everyone else what they want to do." The sheriff suggested. To be fair, it was his mother's idea to have the public vote; of which she liked to say that "a mother knows best." What he didn't tell her was that he had also come to the same conclusion, and thought it should be up to the people of the town to decide.

"That will only give our newspaper more to print on their blasted pages!" Cried the mayor. Having been burned by the editor and chief countless times before, he did not relish giving the paper more fuel for the political fire. "The last thing this town needs is for everyone to come together and start spouting out conspiracy theories as to what is going on here!"

"I second the motion." Archie bravely voiced. "The people are already conjuring up their own explanations. If we come clean with what all we know, then maybe they won't feel as though we are trying to cover something up."

"So…Deputy Becker…are you going to be the one to tell a frightened group of people that you are no closer to solving these recent disappearances as the original officers were over twenty years ago?! How well do you honestly believe that is going to go down?" The mayor added. "The people will have your heads on a spit if something isn't done soon."

"I will be the one to tell them." B.J. rose from the chair with a firm stance. "That's why I have the title, is it not? It's my duty to tell them plainly what is happening, and ask them where we go from here. As of now, I am inclined to enact a strict curfew of five o'clock for the safety of our town. But I will leave it up to them to decide…if that is alright with everyone here on the town council?"

The mayor gave a glance around the sparsely decorated room and watched nearly all of their heads nod in unison. "Very well. A meeting will be called for this evening around four forty-five p.m. We will get signs printed off and posted in all of the businesses in town." With a simple wave of dismissal, the meeting was officially declared over, and B.J. led his deputy down the stairs toward the first floor.

"Bobby Joe, are you sure about this?" Archie inquired from behind his boss's back.

"Of course I am. You supported the notion, didn't you?"

"And I still do. I just don't want your job to suffer if the meeting doesn't go well. You know how spiteful that old badger of a mayor is."

"Then let the chips fall where they may. I did not sign up for this post for the political advantages." B.J. called to Beau, who had been lying on his bed, and radioed for Eric to report his findings when he came back in from patrol. Once his deputy responded over the air waves, B.J. picked up his coat from the rack near the door. "Archie, make sure that Eric files his notes properly this time."

"Where will you be?"

"I'm heading out to do a little more investigative work of my own." The sheriff opened the door and watched Beau race out to his truck, impatiently waiting to be let in. "You can reach me at my mother's house. But I have an errand to run first."

Ten minutes had flown by as B.J. stopped his truck in front of a blue painted bookshop that was owned by Mrs. Healy. He parked along the curb, told Beau to stay in the vehicle, and clambered onto the sidewalk where another batch of discarded potatoes were scattered around the entranceway. The sheriff merely stepped over their frozen skins and walked inside the cozy building. As he passed over the threshold, a small bell resting above the hinges alerted the owner to his presence.

"Coming!" Mrs. Healy's bouncing curls could be seen through the densely populated shelves that consumed the entire first level of the building. Her sweet tone of voice wove with her as she jogged through the maze to see who had just come into her store. "Oh, B.J.!" She smiled at the sight of the sheriff's face staring back through his winter gear. "The cold sure is not letting up this year."

"That's the truth." Seeing movement out of the corner of his eye, B.J. moved swiftly out of the way so a family of three could enter. He waited until Mrs. Healy was finished greeting the new customers before explaining where his companion was. "Beau's in the truck."

"I was about to ask." Her pink lips, which were slightly chapped from tending to the trash earlier that morning, cracked a grin while looking outside at Beau. "I wish I would have known you were coming. I'd have gladly made you some lunch to eat…and a special treat for that golden friend of yours."

"Oh, I know you would. But I'm actually here on an official matter." The sheriff quickly ushered her into the back room, where the family could not listen in on their conversation, and asked her what her opinion was on the festival going forth as planned. He briefly told her what the town council had discussed and the emergency meeting they were calling for that night.

"Deary me!" Mrs. Healy blankly stared at the organized shelves to her right. The books were arranged in alphabetical order by author's last name, with the first novel's focus being on cryptozoology in mountainous terrain. She turned to face her son's childhood friend, wondering why he asked for her opinion of all people. "Are you asking me because I am one of the vendors?"

"Precisely. You have been there every year, and even during the last batch of disappearances. None of the other vendors have attended as many."

"Meaning I'm old."

"Just more experienced." B.J. re-worded. "And growing prettier with each passing minute too…I might add."

"Flattery will get you nowhere with me, Young Man!" She smiled from ear to ear. "Still, it is nice to see you try." Mrs. Healy allowed a short sigh to escape her mouth, placing a wrinkled hand on the shelf that was mounted at chest height. "As for my answer, I'd have to say that the festival should continue like normal."

"What?!" B.J. blinked in astonishment. He thought she would be his best chance at having someone on his side to either enact the curfew or postpone the festival. It was a move he did not relish making, however, it made the most logical sense in the interest of public safety.

"I realize that my answer may not have been what you wanted to hear B.J. But this town could do with some holiday cheer. Think about it; if we allow the darkness to keep us from any potential joy of the season, then it has already won. We cannot live in fear our entire lives." She placed a comforting hand on his arm and smiled her sparkling blue eyes at him. "Is there any way that a few extra deputies could be put on the force for the festival?"

"There are a few I have on standby…" The sheriff stopped himself short at the sound of a bell ringing out by the register. Both of them left the back room and B.J. bid Mrs. Healy farewell as she went to answer a question in regards to an edition of *The Christmas Carol* for a ten-year-old's birthday. Leaving the store, B.J. nearly stepped right onto one of the discarded potatoes, which was not the first time her neighbor had put his trash in front of her place. After writing a third littering fine for Mr. Topfer, the owner of The Dutch Diner, B.J. was happy to get back to Beau waiting for him in the truck.

"Are you ready to go home for a quick visit, Bud?" Once his owner was seated behind the wheel, Beau gladly placed his head atop the sheriff's arm and wagged his tail as the engine roared to life.

They were half-way across town when the snow started up again and B.J. thought back to the other missing persons. In each case, only one thing was left behind; another pair of shoes had been abandoned, a book was dropped open to page twenty-five, and a scarf had been found hanging from a holly bush. No witness saw or heard anything out of the ordinary, no prints had been discovered at the scenes, and all of them occurred near the construction expansion. The only remotely out of place thing was extremely large dips in the snow. There were even various signs posted about town with warnings not to go near the new builds, making it troubling as to why the people had ventured too close in the first place. *And each of them was connected to those who disappeared the last time.*

B.J. had asked *The Harking Herald* to suppress that bit of information from their articles on the fourth day of vanishings, and owed the paper a huge favor in return. Although he felt it was worth the sacrifice to keep that small detail out of the public's eye, they soon realized it anyway. He sensed his mother had figured it out by the third victim; especially after she began telling him to be more careful as of late. There was also an undeniable tension in the air whenever someone who was deemed to be at "high risk" would walk into a store. All of the conversation died once they were inside, and the others would stare at them as though they were a plague. *This has to stop!*

Beau barked when he almost bypassed his mother's house due to being lost in his own thoughts. "Whoops! Thanks for catching that." B.J. backed up, parked, and walked to the porch just as his cousins swung the door open to great him with a big hug.

"We thought we'd never see you again!" Liza exclaimed with her eyes partially watering.

"What are you talking about?" B.J. tried pulling his cousins away, but their grips were too tight to get water through. "Nothing is going to happen to me. You hear?"

Adriana slapped her sister in the arm. "We weren't supposed to say anything, remember?"

"Yeah, that's right." Liza tried to dry her eyes as best she could and looked up at her older cousin with a wide smile. "Great Aunt Eve read us the poem 'Twas the Eve Before Christmas' today!"

"It was called 'Twas the Night Before Christmas,' Liza. Not the *Eve!*" Adriana corrected her twin sister with a smugly drawn grin on her face. She also took another slap to her sister's side for good measure.

"Hey, hey! There is no call for that kind of behavior." B.J. instructed.

"That's enough!" The sheriff's mother stepped out from the kitchen and scolded the girls for their conduct from across the room. "No one is getting another cookie until you clean the mess in the sink. Now get in here and wash up. We need to make sure the house is perfect for when your cousin Norma Jean arrives on the train tomorrow."

"Awww!" The girls cried in unison before giving Beau a few pats on the head and dashing off to tackle a pile of dishes with a towel and some soap.

As soon as the door closed to the kitchen, Mrs. Coppersmith walked briskly toward her son to give him a good looking over. She then placed her left hand directly under her chin and then squinted her eyes as though attempting to read very fine printed text. "What's wrong? That face is sure to fall straight through the Earth if you'd allow it. Something to do with your sister, is it? Will be like old times when she comes home for the festival tomorrow."

"That sounds comforting." B.J. sarcastically replied. "Although, that is not the problem." He was speechless for a moment, unsure how to say it. Growing up, his parents had taught him that it was better to be straight to the point when words failed. Hearing that small voice in his head still didn't make the situation any easier though. "I think I need to enter Father's study."

"Why? Nothing in there except for old papers that are worth less than the ink printed on them." Eve choked back what she really wanted to tell him. "Besides, the girls were looking forward to you joining us for dinner tonight."

"I'm afraid I am going to have to take a raincheck. The council has called an emergency meeting at town hall to discuss the future of the festival at four forty-five p.m. I have no idea how long it will go." B.J. tilted his head towards his mother and firmly held out his hand. "The key." He was not taking "no" for an answer.

Eve reluctantly sighed and detached a small brass object from her ancestor's chatelaine. She silently watched B.J. make his way down the hall and open the room that had been shut for decades. Part of her wanted to remain a statue, holding her breath until her son rejoined her in the main section of the house. But the girls were calling her name from the kitchen and she feared more for the safety of her dishware. Her heels sharply turned as she went back into the battle zone and left her son in silence.

The sheriff hesitantly clicked the light switch on, waiting for the bulb to gain a steady beam of light before he took in the scene before him. His father's desk was as scattered and disorganized as he remembered, with a secret method to the madness only his father ever knew. Pens were perched in a small cup that a friend had purchased from a talented artist at the market many moons ago, and an old lamp with Tiffany-stylized designs sat in the same corner where the sun never seemed to reach. While there were not a lot of genuine antiques being harbored in the cluttered space, everything there had a purpose and a story to share.

B.J. didn't realize how deep in a memory fog he truly was, until the sound of Beau knocking over a stack of papers brought him back to the present. "You better stay in the hall, Bud." He motioned his hand at the doorway, to which his dog begrudgingly obeyed.

Stepping over downed folders and a knocked over trash bin, B.J. carefully maneuvered over to a floppy chair and began to dive into his father's old papers. There were plenty of manuals detailing out the various car models currently driving up and down their town's roads, magazines on upcoming movies, and old Wild West dime novels. A few pencil shavings were dispersed amongst the limited openings on the desk, and a vintage Christmas card from before 1900 was peacefully sitting next to a shabby pair of scissors. B.J. reached for the seasonal card, complete with an illustration of a wreath and candy canes, when the folded paper underneath it caught his attention. *The map he had been searching for the night he went missing!*

B.J. opened the map with his father's handwritten notes that expanded upon his grandfather's findings. He remembered hearing all of the noise from his bedroom that particular evening, as his father searched through his things like a dog after a beloved bone. It was right after his mother had cleaned the space, much to her husband's annoyance, and he'd spent hours looking for the map that told him where to find "The Beast."

"It is not your fault, Bobby Joe." Eve's voice suddenly cut through the silence as she stood in the threshold to the room. "He went out there willingly…on a fool's errand."

"I pushed him, though. Told him that there was no such thing as Krampus, or whatever creature everyone blamed. And that he could not convince me otherwise." B.J. had never spoken about this to anyone before. Storing up all his guilt had caused him to create the lie that his father moved to the other side of the mountain for a new life. The grief had been too much for his younger self to deal with, and he kept on wishing that his fictional version was truly what happened.

"You did not force him to go out there that night, B.J. He went on his own free accord…which will forever be his decision *alone*." Mrs. Coppersmith leaned against the left wall as she went on to confess her own secret. "When Sheriff Bell came to the house, and told us what happened, I didn't answer all of his questions because of how it would reflect upon you."

"Me? I do not understand."

"The town council had approached your father and asked him to help in stopping the monster, because he claimed his family's map held the location to the cave it used to reach Yuletown. And he did in fact find it…or at least said he found it. I never saw the entrance for myself. But he told me that he discovered a larger than life tool near the construction site where the Community Center now stands. He called me to say that he was supposed to meet up with Hans Schmidt at the site, who was his best friend at the time, as another eye witness to the discovery."

"Hans Schmidt?" B.J. wasn't sure what to make of this new information. He never recalled Hans being very close to his father. "Why didn't you tell Sheriff Bell?"

"Because if word got out about your father seeing a gigantic tool before he vanished, then you and your sister would have been treated poorly in school by the other kids. Can you imagine if they had heard about it? Not to mention what the rest of the town would have said; having the 'crazy man' as your father."

It was probably more for my sister's benefit than for me. B.J. thought back to the odd item he'd discovered at the new construction area where Molly had gone missing. A larger than life tool was the perfect description, and he also decided not to let Archie know because of his mother's same reasoning. Suddenly, it was becoming a little more clearer as to what his next move would be. *I have a feeling I know what I have to do. Let's just hope that I have the guts to do it.*

Chapter 8

Sisters Are a Nightmare...Most of the Time

Much to the sheriff's dismay, the townspeople agreed to allow their Annual Christkindl Market to continue on as scheduled. As a fellow Yuletown resident, he always looked forward to the music, food, and wonderful vendors that made the season all the more cheerful. But since it was his duty to keep everyone safe, it pained him to have it continue on with the knowledge that someone else might go missing in the midst of the celebration. *At least I have my job for the time being.*

However, no matter how many times he tried to figure out a way for seven officers to successfully guard the entire festival, which included the four extras sworn in for the three days of the event, he still came up short. There were always gaps without coverage for an hour or two, and unless every single officer worked 'round the clock for seventy-two hours straight, holes were bound to happen. Someone had to be there to supervise the small sheds that were dropped off along Main Street, and be there to secure the vendor's items overnight. The massive headache and weight of responsibility he was carrying clouded his mind; and that was without factoring in his sister's impending arrival.

"Could you drive a little faster? Her train will be due at the station here soon and I don't want to miss it!" Eve demanded. She was jittery with excitement and wanted nothing to go wrong for her daughter's big return home.

"I am not going to drive above the speed limit, and you cannot blame me if we're late. As I recall, I was at the house fifteen minutes earlier than you asked me to be." B.J. was regretting the fact that he agreed to take his mother to the train station at all. Since the moment she entered his truck, her mouth had yet to stop moving, and it was only in the safety of his own thoughts did he find any shred of peace.

"Well, if you had painted the house like you said you would…this *past* summer, then I wouldn't feel so much pressure to have everything look perfect on the inside." She huffed, ranting on about how long it took for her to arrange the pillows on the couch and how she had fallen behind on dusting the mantel with the cousins being around so much.

B.J. was about to speak, and then instantly decided against it. He had learned it was best not to start down that slippery slope with his mother long ago. When it came to his older sister, Norma Jean, his mother held a soft spot in her heart that also blinded her from the faults B.J. clearly saw. For some reason, she always seemed to forget how his big sister bullied him throughout their childhood, and how she nagged him to go to college on the other side of the mountain. "It will be more fun," she said. "You will love the new technology that is all over the place." While he had nothing against those who enjoyed their microwaves talking to them, B.J. was good right where he was. Now, if his sister would accept his decision, it would be a Christmas miracle.

Turning toward the station, B.J. had barely parked the truck before his mother jumped out of the passenger side like a giddy school girl. She thought back to the last seven years her daughter promised to come home for the holidays without keeping it. Leaving her son behind in the blink of an eye, she rushed to the platform with a feeling that it would be different this year; a feeling she swore to be deep in her bones.

B.J. quickly snapped a leash on Beau and hurried after his mother to join the other families who were impatiently awaiting the train's arrival from Connector Station. It sure was a beauty; their town's only steam engine which was fondly nicknamed "Merry Merrill." Having serviced the soldiers with supplies during the Civil War, and carrying cargo before that even, the old locomotive was a workhorse that never quit for the Yule Tide Railroad and Company. Traveling to the station located near the base of the mountain, the passengers would walk off one of the newer models and step into another world on No. 5784.

Their company still relied on paper tickets that the conductors would hand punch, while the other crew members preferred digital passes on phones that sometimes died from a lack of battery power. The steam engine's crew liked the fact that their section of track had no cell service, as opposed to the free internet hookups installed on the modern versions. Both sides learned to co-exist as best they could, managing to stay out of each other's way most of the time. Still, a friendly rivalry was good for business between the two lines, and some of the more frequent passengers ended up dubbing the station as the "Final Standoff" in good fun.

Eve could hear one of the other families whispering to each other, wondering if their relative remembered to charge her phone this time around. But she didn't care; all she wanted to see was her daughter coming down from the passenger car with a pretty smile spread wide across her face. Straining her neck in vain to see around the bend in the tracks, Mrs. Coppersmith wished the tall pine trees would simply move out of her way. "I am so glad we made it here in time. You know, Bobby Joe, I would not put it past you to have deliberately driven like an old man in order to delay when we got here."

"Yes, Mother." B.J. shook his head and felt his nerves stand on end as the sound of No. 5784's whistle pierced the otherwise calm air. He saw the excitement on his mother's face bubble up like a geyser, and dreaded the inevitable disappointment she would try to hide when his sister would not be on the train. "If I were you, Mother, I wouldn't get your hopes…"

"She is going to be on that train, Bobby. Have a little faith." Eve ignored her son and walked away from his negativity just as the nose of Merry Merrill came toward the platform's corner. Everyone backed away from the billowing smoke that was beginning to linger around them, and waited for the metal wheels to completely stop before coming in any closer. The conductor called for the passengers to begin disembarking, wishing them well and helping them down the steps with their luggage.

B.J. did a double take when he saw Norma Jean's large smile appear from the last car at the end. Never in a million years did he actually think she was going to come home for Christmas. He guided Beau into the thicker part of the crowd, hearing him barking at a few of the strangers milling about. It seemed as though the train had been packed with passengers this time, as the platform filled with people of all shapes and sizes in a matter of seconds.

"There she is! There she is! My little angel has come home!" Eve called out to her daughter with a few teary drops in her eyes. "And look how beautiful you've become!"

"Mama!" Norma Jean embraced her mother in a long hug. It wasn't until they separated from one another, did she see her brother and his dog standing behind them. "Little Brother! It's been a long time!"

"Yeah. It's been a year or two…or seven." B.J. awkwardly offered his hand for her to shake, but his sister rushed right up to him and wrapped her arms around his bulky jacket.

"Bet you didn't expect that!" Norma Jean whispered in his ear. "Don't worry. I haven't changed that much. Still going to boss you around like before…Ol' Timer."

And here we go. B.J. forced a grin onto his face as his sister stepped away and reached down to give the golden retriever mix some attention. "I don't think so. See, I'm the one who's in charge around here now."

"Oh I heard. You're the new *town sheriff* and 'The Beast' has returned under your watch." She smirked while scratching Beau's chin with her left hand.

B.J. gave his dog a sideways glance as his furry companion was thoroughly enjoying it. *Man's best friend.* "My deputies and I will take care of it."

"I don't see how. Sheriff Bell had a lot more experience on the force than you, and he couldn't solve the case back then." Norma Jean lifted her luggage up and held it out for her brother to take it to his truck. "But I wish you well."

Clearly, time on the other side of the mountain had not improved his sister's manners at all. B.J. grabbed ahold of her medium-sized suitcase and pointed at the red sweater she was wearing. "It appears that you have arrived in ugly sweater fashion."

"And I have one for each of you! My bestie makes them around the holidays…and I asked for her to make two special ones for both of you to wear at the tree lighting tonight!"

Her sweet-looking expression did not fool her brother. The longer he watched her mischievous eyes staring at him, the more he was relieved to have a work excuse so he could escape her evil plan.

"Shucks! I have to be on duty, so I can't wear it this evening. However, I will see you two there while I'm watching the crowd." Turning to leave, B.J. was about to head toward the parking lot when his sister called his name to stop.

"Oh, that's not all of my things." She used her thumb to gesture toward the baggage car where an unfortunate porter was struggling to unload her other two suitcases.

It's only for a few weeks. It's only for a few weeks. B.J. kept his mouth shut and merely smirked back with a hidden tone of frustration peeking through. While his mother brought Norma Jean up to date with their younger cousins and the multiple baking experiments in her kitchen, B.J. handed the porter a tip in exchange for his help in loading his sister's belongings into the truck. Beau supervised, of course, and happily jumped inside with the rest of the sheriff's family.

B.J. swore he would not give his dog any additional treats that day, and started up the engine so they could return home with enough time for him to get to work. Not surprisingly, the trip back felt much longer than the drive to the station did. His mother and sister were talking about what the city was like, her job as a social media expert, and the fact that she now had a cat living in her apartment called "Gigabyte," or "Gigi" for short. Most of Norma Jean's explanations meant nothing to their mother, who didn't even have a television in her house. But she smiled, nodded, and pretended to understand what a post was, how point-to-click ads worked, and how a video could bring in shoppers through reviews. At least she could relate to podcasts, as they were basically radio shows people listened to on different devices.

The sheriff continued to keep his thoughts to himself, drifting between the disappearances and his security problems for the festival that evening. His deputy, Eric, had been assigned to oversee the setup of the sheds that housed the different vendors, and his other deputy, Archie, was in charge of directing traffic. He even had the mayor promise to keep his speech short for the tree lighting, after nearly putting everyone to sleep the previous year. And Mrs. Healy was given her usual task of decorating the tree with Mont helping her out on the ladder. As far as the rest of the town was concerned, it was going to be a wonderful night filled with laughter and music from the pride of their area, Müller's Oompah band.

"Is Mrs. Healy still at the bookshop?" Norma Jean poked her brother in the side when he didn't respond.

"Huh?"

"I asked if Mrs. Healy was still operating the bookshop."

"Yeah. She runs it by herself right now."

"Good. 'Cause I was hoping to buy some books before going home and it wouldn't be the same without her expertise in mysteries. I heard about this one that was very good, *The Ghost of Christmas Pastel*, and wanted to get her take on it. It's by an author I don't recognize."

"Don't you have some device that holds your stories for you?" Their mother inquired.

"I do. But I miss the feeling of holding a book at times… and actually turning the pages. It's also easier when I want to go back and check on any clues I might have missed." Norma Jean picked at the nail on her index finger and wondered if she should have chosen the color purple rather than pink for her polish. "So…are you worried that 'The Beast' might take you away too?"

"NORMA JEAN!" Eve shouted. "Why would you bring up such a thing?!"

"Because I still subscribe to *The Harking Herald* and even a duck can figure out that all of the new victims are connected to the first victims."

"It's fine, Mother. Nothing is going to happen to me." B.J. slowed down at the next intersection and turned right. He was growing quite tiresome of people worrying about him, but he kept reminding himself that at least he had others who cared. "Should I be touched by your concern for my wellbeing?"

"I just don't want any ol' Beast taking my brother to his dirty cave. It's my job to make your life a living misery, and I'm not very good at sharing!"

Ain't that the truth, B.J. muttered in his head; joking that perhaps being taken away wouldn't be such a bad thing after all.

Chapter 9

Oh, How Tall the Christmas Pyramid

The band was in full swing down the side street, with their Lederhosen and Tyrolean hats partially visible under their winter jackets, as tempting smells of delicious food wafted in the air from various vendors. Both delectable goodies from the Old Country, such as Baumstriezels…also known as chimney cakes…and more American desserts like crumble apple pie were available to shoppers of all ages. Under a green canopy next to the birch beer, pretzels were being formed by skillful hands as the younger kids stood watch at the counter selling Shoofly pies in both wet and dry-bottom options. Burgers could be purchased near the front entrance to the Market, where a hot chocolate stand was busy tending to their long line of customers.

B.J. walked on the sidewalk behind the back of the sheds, making his way swiftly over to where the crafting vendors were located. Painters and chainsaw carvers consumed about a third of Artisan Lane, as the rest of the "small shops" housed a bit of everything else. There were quilters with their blankets and wraps, egg shell carvers with delicate designs atop hollowed chicken eggs, and even an artist with intricate cloisonné jewelry and vases. True pieces of art in all different versions were being purchased by people who came from both sides of the mountain. It was truly a joyous occasion to witness, and the sheriff secretly hoped there would be no trouble that evening.

Inside the historically preserved barn, a German-vaulted ceiling still in its prime, a cookie contest was underway with their town's expert in pastries, Mrs. Anthony. Besides helping to feed the less fortunate at the Community Center, and owning a cat that despised Archie Becker, she also operated a pastry shop on the opposite side of town from the Wagners. When she first opened her doors fifteen years ago, there was a little rivalry that flamed between the two businesses. Molly saw the potential for both of them to thrive in town, but her brothers did not share her open-minded viewpoint.

"Have your hands full with the crowd this evening?" Mrs. Anthony smirked a little when she realized she'd caught the sheriff off guard and interrupted him from examining a batch of snickerdoodles awaiting judgement.

"Nothing our department is not equipped to handle." B.J. answered as confidently as he could, trying to keep his doubts from showing through the facade.

"She wasn't going to go through with the marriage proposal." Mrs. Anthony abruptly said, forcing the sheriff to rack his brain on what she was suddenly referring too.

"You mean Molly?"

The cookie judge nodded. "I talked to her about it the night she disappeared. She had told me that Ferdinand would not accept her rejection, and that Angus demanded she go through with it." Mrs. Anthony took a pause to rearrange a plate of sugar cookie cutouts that were not up to her standards for display. "Molly had her own apartment for a time. But she gave it up and moved back home to help pay off Angus's debts. They didn't deserve her, you know."

"Is Angus into sports gambling?"

"The stock market is more like it. Oh, I realize he is still into sports, and does an occasional bet here and there. But he poured a lot of their family's earnings into a bad venture they hope to dig themselves out of before the bank forecloses on their business." She took a step back from her handiwork and visually approved the now symmetrical plate. "I overheard her tell Ferdinand that she loved another man instead, on the phone from the Community Center. There really was no one else though. Molly was as independent as they come. But it was the only thing left she could think of to stop him from pursuing her."

"Did she tell him who the fake other man was?"

"Timmy Payton." Mrs. Anthony's voice took on a new-founded heaviness as she spoke. "I was going to come forth and tell you sooner. That was until the others…well…the others also disappeared. It was beginning to sound more and more as though 'The Beast' really did return to our town. However," the cookie judge crossed her arms in front of her chest, "I'm still not convinced that he isn't involved in one way or another."

"You think that Ferdinand has harmed the others in order to disguise his real intent of getting even with Molly and Timmy?" B.J. wondered aloud.

Mrs. Anthony merely shrugged her shoulders with indifference. "I wouldn't dream that he was capable of being a kidnapper or a killer. Still, plenty of people commit the wrong acts for many reasons they deem to be right. And we don't ever truly know some townsfolk. Do we?"

Just then, one of the volunteer organizers had come looking for the judge to begin her taste testing of the Fruit-Inspired Category, leaving the sheriff alone with his thoughts and additional questions which remained unanswered. He quickly walked away from the barn, marched past an enlarged nutcracker, and made his way over to where the Schmidts were advertising one of the cars from their lot. Archie had visited with Hans and his son earlier that same day to inquire about the discreet proposal to Molly, and none of what Mrs. Anthony told him was mentioned in his deputy's report. B.J. was determined to find out why they withheld that information, as well as anything else that might have "slipped their minds" during Archie's chat.

Finding Ferdinand without his father by his side, B.J. pushed him back toward the sidewalk and demanded to know if what Molly told him on the phone was true. In what a court of law would have considered "under duress," Ferdinand admitted to the conversation he had with Molly from the Community Center the night she vanished. He also confirmed her "confession" to loving Timmy instead of him and stated that he was going to drop the matter altogether. "I would never hurt her or anyone else!" Ferdinand nearly shouted out of fear, grabbing some attention from the closest patrons. B.J. quickly digressed, and curtly thanked Han's son for his cooperation as he slowly moved away.

No sooner had he left the quivering car salesman behind, did Deputy Becker appear on his left with concern plastered on his face. "What was that all about?"

"He lied to us, Archie. The little fink lied to us." B.J. conveyed what he learned from Mrs. Anthony with a scowl on his lips. "If this bloody town would not have been so caught up in preparations for this dang festival, they might have been more helpful in finding their loved ones!"

He tried checking with the phone and utility companies a few days before, and was told they had no information to provide. B.J. also talked with the closest residents who lived near each of the sites where one of the people went missing. It seemed that no one saw or heard anything that would aid in their investigations, and they were no closer to finding them then when Molly first disappeared. *It is so frustrating...beyond all belief...that they are more wrapped up in their own lives...*

"You realize that they are more scared than anything, right? They don't want to be involved and potentially become a victim themselves." Archie stated, breaking into his boss's internal thoughts. "Now I know that it doesn't make the situation any better, believe me. We just have to keeping trying. That's all we can do."

"Tomorrow morning, we are going to go back and re-question everyone again. If Ferdinand lied to us about a woman he supposedly loved, then who else might have without knowing any of the victims?" However much the sheriff remained slightly skeptical of anyone's testimony, it didn't negate the feeling of betrayal whenever someone withheld vital information.

"CAN I HAVE YOUR ATTENTION PLEASE?!" A gentleman's booming words blared from nearby the Christmas pyramid in the center of the festival. "THE CHRISTMAS TREE LIGHTING WILL BEGIN IN FIFTEEN MINUTES!"

"Sheriff Coppersmith!" Norma Jean's voice floated above the crowd's heads as she led their mother through the densely populated street.

Oh no! B.J. pretended to be delighted to see his sister and asked her if she remembered Archie from her days in school.

"Oh my, yes! I loved your science class when I was in fifth grade."

"Sis, he taught music in second grade." Her brother corrected.

"Right…" Norma Jean failed to cover up her embarrassment with a toothy smile. "Sorry about that."

"That's okay, Miss Coppersmith. I often get confused with my brother, Philip, who did teach that class." The deputy tipped his hat to both of the ladies before excusing himself in order to return to his assigned post beside the whoopie pies; a task he thoroughly enjoyed.

"We came for a closer look at the Pyramid." B.J.'s sister explained. She hooked her right arm through her brother's while wrapping her left arm around their mother. "It's even better than I remember it!"

Four tiers of wooden scenery were beautifully designed in a decorative pyramid with rotating blades at the top. Starting from the bottom layer, and moving on upward, it told of the nativity story and sported large electric candles on the outcropping ends. Traditionally, they were real candles; much like the versions people could order from a local craftsman, as the heat from their lit tips would propel the blades to turn. Nowadays, a mechanical motor was hidden within the pyramid's interior structure that caused the blades' movement. The real burning candles had become a potential safety issue that fueled lively debates even after the change to electric occurred approximately eight years ago.

Due to the camels and the colorful garments worn by The Three Wise Men, B.J. had always had a special interest in that particular tier. Overall, the entire structure was over fourteen feet in height and could be seen from anywhere in the festival. It was truly the star of their Christkindl Market, drawing all kinds of people in to see it for themselves.

"We are going to head on over to the Christmas Tree lighting. Are you able to come with us?" Eve asked her son.

"I have to check in with Eric anyways, so I might as

well accompany you two." B.J. escorted them through the moving waves of people who were making the trek as well. The mayor was already chatting with a few voters, trying to keep his public relations up for next year's election, and the band was settling into their new chairs as they transferred onto the different stage. "Looks as though Mrs. Healy and Mont really went all out on the decorations this year."

The bookshop owner spotted Eve standing next to B.J. and waved from where she stood near the podium. She was finishing up a few minor touches with a couple of red ornaments containing little white dots on all their sides. Mont was in the middle of hooking up the electrical lines for the big moment when the mayor would push the button for the lights to turn on. In the distance, the sheriff found Eric keeping watch by the pet shop as he studied the faces gravitating toward the large tree. Once he caught sight of his boss in the midst of the crowd, the deputy gave him a quick nod of his head.

B.J. left his sister and mother behind at the statue of an author located near Town Hall as he checked in with Eric on how things were going. Their backs were turned only for a moment, when screams erupted from the women standing closest to the alley on their left. The sheriff whipped his head around just in time to see a flash of orange disappear in the direction of the construction site. Dust was beginning to settle around a fallen pretzel while the other people instinctively ran away from the spot.

Panic ensued before the mayor hastily grabbed ahold of the microphone and yanked on the cord to get Mont's attention. With a thumbs up that everything was good-to-go, the mayor fell back on what he did best; talking. Attempting to calm the people with a false sense of security, B.J. and Eric raced past the pretzel and down the alleyway. The same perfume-like smell was faintly present, and B.J. suddenly wished he had Beau with him to follow the trail. For the next several minutes, the duo found themselves chasing shadows until they reached the same location where Molly's boots had been discovered.

"Where's Beau when you need him?" Eric asked, nearly out of breath.

"I left him at the station because he has a fondness for pies." B.J. clicked his flashlight on and swept the beam around the area, where his eyes kept returning to the darkened path leading into the woods. There was something about it he couldn't quite explain; as though he felt an inner draw to enter the looming trees far ahead. But he hadn't been able to decipher his father's notes on that part of the map yet, and dreaded rushing in blindly. "Best we head back and try to find out as much as we can from the witnesses."

Motioning to his deputy that there was nothing more they could do, B.J. was thankful to be surrounded by the festival's lights once again. His extra deputies had joined the mayor in calming the crowd down, and were already setting up a perimeter around the discarded piece of food. The sheriff was about to begin questioning the two women who were closest to the incident just as Archie ran up to him, barely able to speak.

"Archie, what's wrong?!" B.J. was almost frightened by the worried look on his deputy's face.

"It's my brother…Bobby Joe," Deputy Becker wheezed as he tried to catch his breath, "my brother…he's gone! He was supposed to meet me at the Christmas Pyramid a few minutes ago and didn't show. He is NEVER late, ya know. And my sister-in-law told me he left the house over an hour ago. Bobby, I just know something is wrong."

"Could he be the one those two women were screaming

about?" B.J. pointed at the spot in the alley where the partially-eaten evidence remained.

"No, that couldn't have been him. Philip does not like pretzels." Archie seemed to regain most of his breath by then as he straightened his stance. "He hasn't cared for them since he was born."

"Great! That means we have two more people missing now." B.J. flatly stated, struggling to maintain his cool in front of the unsettled crowd. "And this has to end… TONIGHT!"

Chapter 10

Where is Archie's Brother?

B.J. placed a reassuring hand on his friend's shoulder as Beau came jogging up with Eric holding his leash. "We'll find him, Archie. You hear me? We are going to take care of this 'Beast' once and for all." He had never seen his deputy so visibly shaken before; but he figured that it was only natural when someone still looked up to his older brother as his hero. *This breaks with the previous pattern though. No one in his family was ever taken before. Yet another noticeable difference between the two batches of kidnappings.* "Philip wouldn't have ventured near the construction area, right? I mean, there was no reason for him to take such a route."

"Not that I could think of. He should have taken Linden Street and walked down by the drug store like he does every year." Deputy Becker seemed to be a little calmer at the sight of Beau, and patted the dog on the head to steady his nerves. B.J. thanked Eric for retrieving their top-rate sniffer, before they all traced the path Archie described. Leading them towards the drug store, his deputy pointed to the sign marking where Linden Street merged onto Main.

That was when Beau pulled so hard against the leash that it snapped in two, allowing him to run over to where an abandoned cane was lying in an inch of grass and snow. It had been dropped just beyond the road sign and Archie immediately identified it by the odd duck head with a top hat on the handle. Worry lines creased around Archie's face as he stared up and down the street. "I knew it. I knew it! I just knew it! He loves that cane and would never leave it behind…under ANY circumstances. The Beast has him for sure!"

"Easy there, Archie. Let's try to see if he happens to be around here first." B.J. stayed with his dog while the other two surveyed the dark surroundings for any sign of Philip Becker.

Although their surname meant "bakers," Archie's mother was a far better candlemaker than she ever was at making edible dinner rolls. Their family lived on the outskirts of town, where the woods led up to their backyard and the small pond would provide thick-enough ice during the winter for a bit of skating. After both parents passed away, Philip inherited the house; and B.J. secretly wished that the worst case scenario would be his leg trapped within a crack in the ice. But given that his cane was in town, it appeared this was no accident.

Beau kept his nose glued to the ground and began barking at a number of large imprints that were nearly identical to the ones they discovered from a prior night. B.J. was perplexed by the strange markings and wondered what created them. *Could this be the key to solving the mysteries? Or maybe there really IS a beast out there.*

"He is nowhere to be found!" Archie suddenly came rushing back with Eric in tow, both having conducted an exhaustive search of the area. With everyone already at the Christkindl Market, no one was home to ask any questions.

"Alright, what do we know? Most of the victims were

not *small* people…your brother included." B.J. thought back to Philip's past championships as a wrestler before he switched into teaching. While it had been some decades ago, he still carried a bulkier frame as proof of his golden years. "None of the people who were taken have put up a fight, so they were either surprised or did not feel threatened by their attacker. Only one item is ever left behind to even suggest someone has been taken in the first place; indicating that the kidnappers are not interested in covering their tracks." He then pointed out the large indents that Beau had found to the two deputies. "These marks are not very deep, so they couldn't have been made from any heavy equipment or large vehicles. In fact…" His eyes squinted at them in the light from a nearby street lamp. "It almost looks like the handprint my mother sometimes leaves in flour on the counter in her kitchen."

"So it is Krampus who is seeking his revenge on our town?" Eric half-heartedly asked.

B.J. ignored his deputy's question, scratching his barefaced chin that was growing sorely cold from a recent breeze. "This just doesn't add up. How could there be nothing else to go on?" Just then, he noticed Beau looking particularly interested under a bush a few yards away from where they stood. The sheriff wasted no time in joining his dog by the undergrowth and picked up a long white, almost silver, thin strand measuring at about twice his height in length. "What the…?"

"Is it fur of some sort?" Archie voiced.

"A weird piece of rope? Or some new invention, perhaps?" Eric offered.

The sheriff wasn't sure what to think about the strange piece of evidence. "I doubt it belongs to Krampus. That being said, both of you need to return this to the station on the double. And Eric, give me your flashlight."

"What are you going to do?" The deputy took the unidentified item from his boss's outstretched hand, not wanting to ask why he needed a second light.

B.J. pulled his family's folded map from his pocket. "I'm going to nip this whole thing in the bud by finding out if there really is a beast out there; once and for all! You two can take over at the square. Archie is in charge until I return." *If I do return that is.* After checking to ensure that Eric's flashlight had enough battery power, he shoved the light into his back pocket. He didn't wish to repeat a prior incident when his deputy had neglected to put new batteries in before one of his night shifts.

As Beau barked beside his right leg, ready to go off on another adventure with his owner, B.J. regrettably told him it was far too risky and ordered him to stay with Archie. "Aw, Beau…I couldn't live with myself if anything happened to you." He knelt down to give his partner a final hug before handing over half of the leash to Deputy Becker. "Take good care of him."

"Will do. Hey, Bobby?"

"Yeah?"

"What do you want me to tell your mother and sister?"

B.J. hadn't gotten to that step yet in his head; considering he was still trying to figure out what his plan would be if he came face to face with the supposed "Beast." He took a second to think, and then cast his friends a short grin. "Tell them I'll be more careful than a walrus."

Archie and Eric nodded in silent agreement, all the while ushering Beau back toward Main Street against his will. There was nothing more to say between them, as they each understood that this might be the last time they ever saw their boss alive.

Chapter 11

Into the Woods I Must Venture

The swinging branches of the pine trees made the creepiest noise in the dark of the night. Between the massive tree trunks, the cold air swirled around the freezing sheriff, and he could feel his own fear laughing in the back of his mind. There was no escaping the abyss that was known to all as Owl's Hollow, and his father's ramblings were not becoming any clearer the longer he stared at them on the old paper.

According to the map, he had entered the woods at a more southerly point than where Molly had been when she disappeared. It was not the easiest entrance to take, by far, but it also happened to be the most direct route to where his ancestor had marked the cave to be. B.J. pulled his jacket up to his chin and dipped his head against the oncoming wind. Gazing about the high ridge set before him, he tried to find a route that didn't require climbing up the entangled rocks ahead.

The flashlight's beam of light failed to pierce the dark farther than twenty feet in any given direction, which only added to the dooming outlook for his journey to find "The Beast." B.J. continued to switch his attention from the map to the ridge, and back again; desperately searching for a break in the landscape as the cold bit down even harder through his jacket. Unfortunately, there was no visible path he could see that would take him less than two hours out of the way. Not to mention that those routes appeared to lead through windier sections of the woods and the cold was already not his friend.

Rolling up the map and tucking it away inside his jacket for safe keeping, B.J. straightened his back and took in a deep breath. "Right. I guess climbing it is then."

He located some broken branches nearby and used them to angle the flashlight so it faced the thirteen foot wall of wet rock, green vines, and decaying needles dropped by the overhead trees. Starting the climb was the easiest part. Then, about halfway towards the top, he found himself without a clear spot to reach for the next grip. Mountain sports, including climbing and hiking, were not his forte. And latching onto cold stone in the woods after dark was not his idea of a great time to take it up either.

With a deep breath, B.J. forced himself to remain calm and began mumbling to himself not to look below at the plummeting fall he could take to his death. Slowly, and with purpose, he managed to make it near the top edge of the slippery incline. But just as he went to pull down on a large outcropping, the rock suddenly gave way under his hand and adrenaline instantly pumped into his veins.

Feeling much of his strong hold being yanked out from underneath him, B.J. strained his other arm to cling to whatever part of the ledge he could find. Dirt and gravel gave way, rolling through the harsh shadows cast by the flashlight on the ground before ultimately colliding with his only source of light. The world went dark all around him as he hung on for dear life, and his frustrations kept mounting from the inside. Now stranded on the ridge, B.J. believed an attempt to reach the light in his back pocket would be too risky. "If only I could see what I was doing!"

After ten more minutes of grappling with small debris, wet rock, and falling greenery, B.J. was finally able to crest the top and rolled onto his back in an uncelebrated victory. His chest heaved from the scare of nearly falling off the ridge, as his body wanted nothing more than to rest for a few minutes. But the sheriff refused to relax so close to the edge of the rocks and quickly picked himself up to plunge deeper into the forest. B.J. didn't slow his pace until he finally felt safe enough to lean against a tree for a short break.

All around him sat the harsh winter landscape as far as his eyes could see. The jagged trees were of little help in knowing where he was, and despite having the brains to ask for a spare flashlight, he failed to bring along a compass. B.J. pulled the map out once again, and grabbed the light from his back pocket. He clicked it on only to find the beam merely flickering at the folded paper. "Come on! Seriously?!" Slapping the light against the palm of his hand, in the hopes that the batteries would work even a little bit longer, the sheriff gratefully smiled when the beam turned solid. "Thank you! Now onto finding that cave."

He warmed his fingers the best he could by blowing on their frozen tips and then fumbled with the paper as his nose began to drip from the cold. B.J. glanced around at the barren bushes and undergrowth that was lifeless in an apocalyptic sort of way. Taking note of a bear-like drawing on the map, he looked up to find a natural rock formation that was very similar in shape. At first, the rock nearly scared him to death in the darkened woods. However, it was not as frightening as the sound of a snapping twig he suddenly heard coming from his left.

B.J. immediately aimed the flashlight's beam in the direction where the sound occurred, but nothing appeared to be there. Standing perfectly still, the sheriff wondered if "The Beast" had found him instead. He listened intently for another sign that something else was out there, trying to tune out the pounding of his own heartbeat that reached his ears. Squinting into the night, the sheriff attempted in vain to catch a glimpse of any more of the white-silver strands his dog had found in town. To his dismay, only the soft dance of a few discarded leaves could be seen in the chilly air.

B.J. wasn't sure what to do. His feet felt welded to the ground, unable to move due to the fear that something was watching him…hunting him…sizing him up to become the next victim from Yuletown. *Get out of your own head! The faster we find the cave, the sooner we will be out of these creepy woods.* Forcing his right foot to move, and then his left, dried leaves crunched under his boots as he walked toward the rock formation. The hairs on his neck were on end as goosebumps shivered down his spine, feeling the weight of large eyes pinned onto his back. He convinced himself to keep walking forward, in the hopes that "The Beast" was not secretively lurking ahead for an unsuspecting meal.

As soon as he made it to the natural rock formation, B.J. peered down at the map with his flashlight beginning to flicker once again. He angrily beat the handle, commanding it to work through a bunch of scared mutterings. That's when a soft swishing sound caused him to freeze in place. His eyes searched his surroundings wildly, remembering the flash of orange he had seen at the tree lighting earlier that evening. *Krampus isn't orange. Is he?*

His ears suddenly picked up on the ever-so-gentle pattern of breathing, which was traveling steadily closer now. B.J. slowly turned his head around to face a pair of enormous green eyes staring back at him, with their pupils being over ten times the size of his own. The sheriff's nose smelled a wave of perfume instantly hit him like a tsunami wave as "The Beast" opened its mouth, ready to devour.

"Please do not eat me." B.J. pleaded. "I'm not here to hurt you, or attack you. I just want to find the others you took from our town. Their families deserve to know what happened to them." *Well, maybe the Wagners don't seem to care. But the others sure do.*

Before he even knew what was happening, the sheriff saw the green eyes close and he felt the unsettling sensation of teeth tightening around most of his body as "The Beast" lifted him from the ground. B.J. shouted for the furry creature to let him go, calling out for help into the remote wilderness that swallowed his words within seconds. B.J. began to think that this would be the end for him; unable to see his cousins again, rub Beau's ears the way he liked, or have his bossy sister try to make him wear a horrible ugly sweater with lights. But, to be honest, he was quite alright without that last one.

Struggling to get free only wore him out faster, as the jaws of "The Beast" were too strong in its unrelenting grip. B.J. succumbed to the fact that there was nothing more he could do than to go along for the ride and see if there would be an opportunity to escape later. He watched the ground speed by him in a blur as the creature's stride was much longer than he could have imagined possible. Daring to look at where they were headed, B.J.'s eyes widened at the sight of the cave that had been marked on the map. *My family was right! The cave is where "The Beast" lives!*

The blackest void awaited them there, while B.J. felt

Eric's flashlight slip from his hand and drop onto the forest floor. There was no point in having his eyes open any longer, as the place was devoid of anything to see. Quietly, in his mind, he prepared himself for the inevitable just as the creature took a steep plunge downward before landing on hard ground once again. It was then that a soft glow hit his eyelids, and B.J. peered out to see a world of light and colors from something out of a dream. His ears detected the sound of human voices from a far-off distance, and he allowed himself to entertain the thought of being saved…until "The Beast" climbed into another darkened hole leading further away from Yuletown.

With what was beginning to feel like an eternity, quickly stopped when B.J. was abruptly dropped onto a floor that was smooth and had little dirt. He shook his head and tried to blink his eyes fully open, staring at a landscape he couldn't quite describe. "The Beast" called out into the still air, from somewhere nearby, and after hearing his "roar" for the first time, B.J.'s jaw dropped open like a drawbridge. *Did it just meow?!*

Chapter 12

And To All A Good Night!

B.J. couldn't believe what he was actually looking at. As "The Beast" took a step into a stream of light shining on his left, a large, and beautiful, orange cat came into view. Her green eyes were now much gentler, with a sort of calming comfort held within her pupils; and her white-silver whiskers shined in the yellow glow of the ceiling light from above. Blinking away what he thought was a hallucination, the sheriff cautiously arose from the ground to take in the sight of their town's "Krampus."

"Bobby Joe?"

B.J.'s heart nearly bottomed out at the sound of the voice that spoke his name. Taking a turn almost so quickly he knocked himself off balance, B.J. watched as an older version of his father rushed toward him in a blur. A nostalgic warmth shot through him when his father's arms wrapped around his jacket, making him remember the seven-year-old boy he had once been. The sheriff no longer felt scared of where he was, or alone in that moment, nor the fear that "The Beast" was eventually going to eat him. Instead, he had never felt happier and filled with such gratitude in his life. "Pop! I thought you were dead!"

"Thought so myself for a time." His father didn't let go for several minutes, holding onto the son he believed he'd never see again. "But this cat is sure different than Coal was."

B.J. was confused, pulling himself out of his father's grasp with a puzzled look on his face. "Coal? Who's Coal?"

"When I was taken from Yuletown, all those years ago, it was because of a nasty cat named Coal who snatched me up and dropped me down here in the Bauer's kitchen. I was lucky to escape his vicious claws and found residence with the others he kidnapped, here behind their refrigerator."

The sheriff was speechless for a spell, merely blinking his eyes as his brain tried to catch up. "What are you talking about? Who's kitchen? Where exactly are we?"

His father inhaled a deep breath and placed both of his hands on his son's shoulders. "This is going to be a lot to absorb all at once…so just remain calm, Bobby Joe."

"Okay?"

"The Bauers used to own the house we are standing in…and the older Bauer loved model trains. Yuletown, and the mountains, and the city on the other side, are all part of his model train setup in the attic. Coal used to be their cat; named after his rotten behavior and the fact he was a present on Christmas morning. That's the year we all went missing, and afterwards, Old Man Bauer shut the door to the attic to keep the cat from going inside."

"We?" B.J. glanced past his father to find a small village with a life force all its own. It was fashioned out of everyday materials that were produced on a bigger scale than B.J. was used to seeing; such as enlarged matchboxes being repurposed as buildings and toothpicks being used to hold up porch roofs made out of moldy pieces of crackers. In the center of the half-circle village was a campfire pit, constructed from the measuring end of a metal teaspoon, were others from Yuletown were currently gathered.

"We." His father stated with definite pride. "All of us survived Coal's wrath and created New Yuletown with our own hands. It didn't take us long to figure out that Coal could not reach behind the refrigerator." Just as he said the word, a loud sound came from the extremely tall electrical appliance and caused B.J. to jump backwards. "Don't worry about that. The ice maker just kicked on."

"So…you're telling me that our town is someone's hobby?!" The sheriff thought the whole thing was not just bizarre, but also pretty far-fetched as notions went.

"It was WAY more than a hobby to Bauer, B.J. However, they weren't able to take our town with them when they moved to Florida to be closer to the grandkids, so they sold the house to Natalia Angelo. She is very nice…despite the fact that she is Italian and not German." His father winked at him before pointing up at the orange feline watching them in quiet contentment. "And this is 'Allegria,' or 'Alli' for short. It means 'joy.' And as you can see, she is a little smaller than Coal was, so she can fit back here. Luckily, she is a very friendly cat indeed."

The dots were beginning to connect for B.J. "That's why there is such a gap in the kidnappings!"

"Exactly. Natalia opened the doorway again, and she loves trains just as much as Bauer did! In fact, our town is part of the reason why she bought this house. She plans on expanding it so the entire attic can become one large train world!" Mr. Coppersmith smiled from ear to ear. "We'll be the best model train display this side of the river. At least that is what Natalia told her mother while they were on the phone. As to which river, we haven't figured that out just yet."

B.J. was still in the midst of trying to grasp the fact that their town was a model setup. "So, are all of the others here? The ones that your 'friendly' catnapper recently stole? Molly…Timmy…"

His father chuckled as he encouraged his son to walk with him. "Relax Dear Boy! They are all here!" He made a sweeping gesture with his hand toward the small town that also included fences out of erasers, lawns fabricated from pieces of old newspapers, and landscaped streets with small stones brought in from people's sneakers. "Alli overheard us talking about how much we missed our families and decided to help by bringing them to us. She didn't do it out of spite. Simply wanted to see us smile, is all." The father-and-son duo continued to talk while making their way over to the campfire.

"Then who wanted to see Archie's brother, Philip? I don't recall their family as being one of the original group that went missing."

Mr. Coppersmith squinched up his face. "Well…that one was an accident. See, Wilhelmina had mentioned missing the jokes that Archie would tell her in class in school, and Alli mistook him for his brother."

B.J. rolled his eyes while thinking back to when his sister had done the same thing at the Market. "Yeah, that does tend to happen…so I hear."

At the sound of his voice, Molly Wagner glanced up from the flames of the fire pit and waved to the sheriff when she saw him approaching. He noticed that her brown hair was pulled back in the pristine bun she always wore, but a pair of new shoes made from scraps of a candy wrapper were around her feet. "We heard Alli call out that she brought another one from town. By the way your father reacted, I figured it had to be a Coppersmith." She shifted her weight back and forth, looking down at her wax-covered boots. "Mr. Dirchs crafted these for me. They may be a little strange in appearance, but I like that they're different. And they fit better than my brother's did."

"Well, I'm just glad to find you're safe and sound. All of you." B.J. counted out the number of people who were keeping warm by the fire, and a flood of relief hit him at seeing that all of the old and new ones were there.

Molly opened her mouth to ask a question, only to hesitate before she said what was on her mind; uncertain if she truly wanted to know the answer or not. "What did my brothers say? When you talked to them?" Her fingers were intertwined amongst themselves in a shy manner. "You did speak with them…right? About my disappearance?"

B.J. cast her a half-smile. *What should I say? No? That your brother was more worried about you marrying Hans' son and Steven inquired about his boots? Do I have the heart to tell her that?* He cleared his throat, trying to cover up his delay in responding to her. "They were concerned in their own way. Reggie's sister was very worried about you, in point of fact."

That seemed to bring the baker a sense of bittersweet happiness to her face. "Grace. She is a good student and a decent human being…who thankfully has more of her mother's traits."

By now, the rest of the group had migrated over to where the trio was chatting, which saved B.J. from having to talk any more about Wagner family issues. All twelve of the original missing relatives happily greeted the sheriff with open arms and told him their memories of when he was little. They had so many questions as to what was going on in Yuletown, about his new position as the sheriff, and whether the Christkindl Market was still being held this year.

B.J. answered as many as he could before holding his hands up for them to give him a break. "Hang on! I do have a question of my own to ask."

"Why haven't we gone back during this whole time?" His father guessed.

"I know one thing for sure. I'd give those two sons of mine a right good kick in the beeehind if I ever get back home." Mr. Wagner interjected. "Molly told me what happened to the bakery, and those two hooligans trying to get her married off to bail Angus out of his own problems! Well no, Sir! Not under my watch!"

"Dad!" Molly placed a hand on his shoulder.

"But that's my point." B.J. stated. "If you all are still here, in the same house, and…undead…then why did you not come home?"

"Because we don't know how." Mr. Dirchs replied from the back of the group. "As we were just telling Philip, here, attempting to locate the attic is too risky. We tried several times in the past and almost got completely lost."

"Why not ask the cat to take us back?" B.J. pointed in the direction to where Alli had been standing during their reunion, and now saw that the feline had completely vanished from view. "Wait…where did she go?"

"She isn't allowed to be in the kitchen when Natalia gets home." Mr. Coppersmith tipped his finger into the air, and as if on cue, the front door opened. A young woman walked into the house and started speaking to the cuddly pet rubbing her legs. "Besides, the only way out of the kitchen is to run across the floor and hope we can make it to the stairs alive. While Coal was here, he would take up guard right beside the doorway as though his life depended upon it. Day or night."

Mr. Dirschs nodded his head. "One time, we almost made it and Mrs. Bauer thought we were fleas that jumped off that miserable feline. So she had someone come in and…how did they say…use 'flea bombs' in the house. I had a terrible cough for two months straight after that; and your father almost died from an infection in his lungs."

"But Coal is no longer here and you all say that this cat is nice, so we could try again."

"We are no spring chickens, B.J." Mr. Wagner answered, gesturing toward his seventy-year-old body with a limp in his stride. "Not that there isn't some life still in these wobbly legs of mine…however, my running days are over. I can still crack a nasty punch though." He chuckled as the others agreed with muttered replies.

"As long as Natalia doesn't see us, we should be good…right?" The sheriff thought aloud, replaying the trip Alli took to get him there in his mind for a spark of inspiration. "I did hear some voices on my way down. Perhaps whoever they belong to would be willing to help us?"

"That was probably a TV show you heard. Natalia tends to leave one of her televisions on for Allegria when she heads off to work for the day." Wilhelmina explained. "And she loves to cook. Spends most of her time in the kitchen to unwind from her job at the flower shop. But she did mention something the other day about having fun putting a fresh batch of snow on Yuletown." Her mind drifted into her memories of Christmas back home. "I always enjoyed the first snow of the season."

"See?! That means that we have a chance to leave right now; before she steps into the kitchen and blocks our escape, or heads into the attic to work on our town. What do you all say?" B.J. gazed about the semi-circle of people blankly staring at one another, each one waiting for someone else to speak first. He didn't understand their hesitation at having a chance to finally go home after all these years. "You don't want to go back?"

Mr. Coppersmith stepped forth with a heavy sigh as he spoke. "Not sure it's that, Son. It's just…well…I've…we've, actually, we've kind of given up on seeing Yuletown ever again. Being away for so long…it feels like another lifetime anymore."

In a sea of nods spread out before him, B.J. could tell that his fellow townsfolk had lost all hope…the one thing more powerful than an ocean of darkness. It was their light-house, their beacon, that drained over the decades of wishing they could return to see their families and friends, until barely ashes remained. *If I can only stoke that fire inside them again...* "It is Christmas, you know. The season for miracles."

Molly glanced around at her neighbor's long faces and decidedly put her foot down when she saw no one else was going to. "He's right, everyone! Look, my brothers may not have treated me fairly this year, but I miss them…regardless. They are our family…and we only have one. So what do you say? Should we give it a final try?!"

Mr. Dirschs was the next to speak up. "I would like to see my daughter again."

"And I do miss all of my cats." Wilhelmina took a step toward B.J. and planted her foot next to Molly. "It's settled. We are all going." One by one, as if they were dominoes, the rest of the townsfolk nodded in agreement, ending with his father's final look of approval.

"Okay, then." B.J. had a feeling that this was going to work. "Follow my lead." He made his way between the side of the refrigerator and the cabinet that housed Natalia's new dishwasher. Surveying the wooden floor sprawled out before them, B.J. kept to the baseboard of the trim and used the overhang of the cabinets as coverage. *I sure hope I know what I'm doing. Who am I kidding?! Of course I have no idea what I'm doing.* He was almost to the end of the cabinets when a certain perfume scent hit his nose again. Looking to his right, a hand-sewn mouse with button eyes and a leather string tail was waiting for Allegria to be in the mood for playtime. *The smell must be some form of catnip!*

Grabbing ahold of the mouse's tail, B.J. asked for each of the younger people to help him drag the fake rodent across the room and over to the stairs. As it so happened, fortune appeared to be on their side while they watched Natalia settle into the living room for a holiday movie on the couch. Once she was preoccupied with a Christmas classic, B.J. led their group along the floor transition strip and kept glancing over his shoulder to check on Mr. Dirsch's bummed knee.

"We're almost there." Molly released her grip on the mouse's pink ear in order to take a break at the bottom of the smooth stairs. "I do hope you have an idea on how we are going to climb these steps that are taller than a skyscraper."

"Hence the mouse." Timmy chimed in from near the mouse's butt, fixing the worn newsboy hat atop his messy hair. "Or were you not listening to what B.J. said before? Me thinks we are to entice a certain cat over here to use as our ticket out."

"Right you are, Timmy." The sheriff looked to his father, who was a much better whistler than he was, and watched Alli's head turn at the unusual sound. Her curious eyes studied her toy beginning to shake on its own accord, and she jumped down to stalk it like prey.

"I sure hope she hurries up here soon!" Timmy strained from under the weight of the stuffed fabric. "This is no light mouse! More like a fat rat, if you ask me."

"Allegria? What are you doing?" Natalia paused the movie in order to look around for her pet.

B.J. immediately ordered them all to stop moving and held his breath in the anticipation of being caught. But when the young florist found her cat stealthily approaching her catnip toy, she shrugged it off and went back to the television without a care in the world. Everyone let out a huge sigh of relief just as the orange-furred feline stared at them with intrigue. "Can you help us get home?"

While he almost wished he could speak cat in that moment, B.J. did not need any translation for what happened next. Alli calmly laid down with her chin resting on the floor so they could all climb atop her back like a horse. The sheriff helped the others to board their furry friend before he did, latching onto the feline's coat near her aqua-colored collar last. He then whispered to her that they were ready and prepared himself for the bumpy return ride home.

Considering that B.J. was not being held captive between Alli's teeth this time around, the trip was much more enjoyable for the sheriff. And the closer they came to reaching their home of Yuletown, the more B.J. could not wait to tell his mother that his father had truly been right. The cave actually *was* the key to the whole mystery, providing evidence that their world was vastly different from what they'd believed it to be their entire lives. This startling revelation should have excited the sheriff to be able to tell his friends and neighbors that "The Beast" was not their Old Country's Krampus. However, when their transport let them off in the woods that made up Owl's Hollow, he suddenly felt more nervous than excited.

They all thanked Alli for her help and watched her

disappear again into the caverns that housed most of the electrical power lines for Yuletown. "Pop?" B.J. pulled his father aside from the others, who were looking about the dark forest with wondrous eyes. "Should we say anything to the rest of the town? I mean…the fact that we are living in a train model display?"

Mr. Coppersmith closed his eyes, tilted his head back, and held his right hand to his chin as he contemplated his son's question. "That is something I have thought about for quite a long while. Perhaps it is best if we continue to keep the story of 'The Beast' alive. Could put a whole damper on the town's mood. Don't you think?"

B.J. tapped his father's shoulder with a grin on his face. "Yeah. I was going to suggest the same thing. Although…we might want to get our statements straight for the mountain of questions they are bound to have for us."

"My sentiments exactly." His father touched the side of his nose with his index finger, instantly reminding B.J. of Montgomery Senior and how he still had to save his job.

"I forgot all about Mont!" As the sheriff was about to explain the situation to his father, something clicked in his own mind. "You know, I think it was Mont who wrote this warning note I found on my truck awhile back." B.J. chuckled half-heartedly to himself, thinking of the way the letters were formed. "He does write left-handed, and I wouldn't put it past him to try discouraging me from getting into any real danger."

"Sounds like I owe Mont more than a few drinks for looking after you so well."

"There is actually something else I had in mind."

"Go on." Mr. Coppersmith listened to his son explain about the council's decision to terminate Mont's employment, right before his eyes lit up with an idea on the matter.

"We can easily take care of that. Don't you worry about him. Montgomery Junior and I have a little unfinished business about an overdue bill on his vehicle. Considering I haven't been at the shop in over two decades, I have a feeling that it slipped many people's minds. Should have racked up a hefty bit of interest on that account, I would say. Might have to make a deal with the grocery store owner in lieu of a cash payment." B.J.'s father shared a smile with his son. "It is going to be a very Merry Christmas this year, My Boy! Yes, Sir. A very Merry Christmas indeed!"

Molly turned away from the view on the top of the cliff to see B.J. chuckling with his father. She was glad for the sheriff that he no longer had to walk around with a cloud of the past hanging over his head. With a soft grunt from her throat, she broke into their conversation to ask a question. "Anyone know how to get down from here?"

"Have no fear, Molly. I have the map to take us home." B.J. and his father moved to the front of the group as they used their family's map to guide them home towards Yuletown; never knowing that they would be taking the same route B.J.'s grandfather did when he returned from adventuring in the Bauer's house. For how did the cave appear on the map in the first place?

<u>Congrats on Completing Your Advent, Fellow Reader!</u>

You can stop here; content in the knowledge that all of the people who were deemed "missing" are going home to their families and looking forward to a Merry Christmas.

OR…

If you are interested in finding out how some of their family reunions went, you can flip the page and continue on to read the "Optional Epilogue."

The choice is yours to make, Dear Reader.

Epilogue

The Family Reunions!

After the group made it safely down the mountainside and entered Yuletown, the place was deserted enough for a tumbleweed to roll across Main Street. Terrified of being the next target for "The Beast," everyone went home as fast as they could from the Christkindl Market. Vendor sheds were closed, locked up with chains and padlocks. The tree was left twinkling in the empty square after a kid pushed the red button while the mayor wasn't looking. It was an eerie sight to behold, as B.J. half-expected to see a pair of gunmen step onto the road in a duel at the stroke of midnight.

Both the sheriff and his father decided to walk the others to their homes, and to remind them all of the storyline they agreed to tell their family members. Here is some of what happened…

The Paytons:

Timmy found Edwina pushing her rocking chair back and forth in her slippers. She had been curled up in the chair with her brother's favorite blanket cradled in her arms, with tear stains running down her cheeks. Once she heard the key turn in the lock, her heartbeat ran faster as she just knew he had returned home. They hugged one another in a sibling embrace, before she slapped him in the shoulder for causing her so much stress; and for having to bring in all the firewood by herself to stay warm.

The Wagners:

Molly and her father opened the bakery to find it cleaned spotless by Reggie and his sister, Grace. The place looked almost exactly how he had left it all those years ago, causing a few tears to form in his eyes. Upon hearing the bell that was left on the counter for customers to ring, Reggie groggily walked down the stairs and blinked his bleary eyes at the two people standing before him. He recognized the one only because his picture was on the wall next to the mixer, and he rushed back up the creaky steps to wake the rest of the family. When Steven and Angus saw their father, a sheepish look filled their eyes as they were scolded for taking advantage of Molly's love for them. Mr. Wagner set the record straight once and for all that she was to make her own decisions in life and Angus had to fix his own mistakes.

The Beckers:

Archie stayed at the police station with Beau, both of them staying wide awake with worry about Philip and Bobby Joe respectively. He had the needle on his record player going over *White Christmas* for the twentieth time that evening as he munched on a cookie Mrs. Healy had left for the sheriff. When the sound of footsteps along the cracked sidewalk prompted Beau to bark, Archie rushed to the door and peered through the mail slot to see his brother and boss steadily approaching. The deputy flung the entrance wide open and gave Philip a hug at the same time Beau jumped into his owner's arms. Philip then asked what had become of his treasured cane, to which Archie answered by fetching it from his desk and gratefully walking his brother home.

Mr. Dirschs and Wilhelmina:

Mr. Drischs returned home to his cobbler's workshop, where his daughter had been singing her newborn to sleep upstairs. She had continued his trade, along with her husband of three years, and his old bedroom was cleaner than the day he went missing. His Christmas was to be bittersweet, as he learned about the passing of his dearly beloved wife seven years before.

His neighbor, Wilhelmina, was happy to discover that her best friend had moved into her house to care for her fifteen cats. Although a few of them had moved on in life, their pictures were hung over the fireplace and their stockings were all set out for Santa Paws to visit on Christmas Eve. There were even a few new feline friends to meet!

And...Last But Not Least...the Coppersmiths:

Having already witnessed the others start returning to their former lives, it was finally time for B.J. and his father to do the same. The sheriff had introduced his furry friend at the station, and the trio hopped into the pickup truck to relieve their aching feet. On their way home, however, Mr. Coppersmith was growing a little fidgety in the passenger seat as worry and doubt began to plague his mind. But with B.J.'s confident encouragement that everything would be fine, he steadied his hands and waited for his son to park in front of the house.

At the sound of the truck's door opening and closing, Eve appeared in the doorway with Norma Jean at her side.

Both women ran down to the curb and embraced B.J., who had a plan on how to ease them into the shock of their lives. That was until his mother caught sight of their father waiting in the truck. Her body went rigid like a stone statue, sensing that there was way more to her son's venture than he was going to let on. When Norma Jean saw her father stepping out into the open, her jaw dropped to the ground in disbelief.

"Well, there went my peaceful life." Eve sharply turned on her heels and went back toward the house, leaving the other three behind in an instant. "Best to come in from the cold or else we'll all be sick for Christmas."

Mr. Coppersmith shared a look with his son. "That went better than I feared it would." B.J. admitted. "On the plus side, Norma Jean can have her friend make you an ugly sweater." He elbowed his sister in the side to bring her back to reality.

"Owww! Do you want a green or blue shirt?" His sister squinted her eyes, studying her father's complexion in the low light. "I think a lime green. And we can add pom-poms with frills and llamas too!" She went over to hug him in a sort of delayed reaction, still trying to process the fact that her father was really the one standing there.

Mr. Coppersmith's eyes widened as they turned to stroll up the porch steps. "That…is an intriguing combination. I must say." B.J. laughed on the way to the front door, where once inside, Eve did give her husband a kiss on the lips and said it was nice to have him home for Christmas…mostly.

<u>**And Since Christmas is the Time
for Giving...**</u>

Please consider the following excerpt as my gift to you!

It is the first chapter of my next book,

In Plein Air Sight
A Cybil Lawson Mystery #2

Coming in 2026

For more information, please visit my website at
www.SarahIckesArt.com

Chapter 1

Twelve Days Ago...

"He is *sooo* dead!" Cybil Lawson exclaimed; looking over at her roommate with shared frustration. Her hands were running through her hair from the dread of what she knew was going to happen. Though she wanted nothing more than to scream at the television with all her might, it wasn't as if the contestants would be able to hear her, so what was the use?

"Aw man! I really wanted him to win!" Yasmin Manahan placed a red slushy straw into her mouth and sucked up the equally red, and quite sugary, drink. There was only a mere few sips left, but she needed to do something in order to keep herself from exploding at the flat screen in front of them.

"Anyone who has ever watched...even *ONE* of these baking competitions...knows that you NEVER make a brownie to serve the judges!" Cybil tossed some popcorn onto her tongue, waiting for the next commercial break in order to grab her cereal bars from the cupboard in the kitchen. Except for the two bedrooms and a bathroom, the converted railroad station they called home was mostly an open plan; so it didn't really matter in a way. But after waiting for so long to see the finale of their favorite spring competition, Cybil didn't want to miss even the smallest fraction of the seasonal show.

Yas finished her drink and placed the empty cup on their new end table. "Do you think that Sydney has a chance with that lemon curd tart she's mixing with those strawberries and a toasted pecan crunch?"

"Depends on what the twist is that the host hasn't announced just yet."

"Awww." Yasmin swayed back and forth on the couch out of impatience. "I really have to go to the bathroom. When's the next commercial break?" No sooner had she asked, then the television station moved to a fried chicken ad and both women jumped up without hesitation.

While they did have a few streaming services they paid for, the Spring Dessert Competition was only aired on the regular stations, and didn't go to "On Demand" until the summertime. Cybil and Yasmin weren't considered to be expert bakers by far, but they still enjoyed watching the contestants battle it out in friendly challenges without the drama of the other reality shows. Learning about foods like dump tarts, pâte à choux, berry compote, and tips such as toasting almonds in order to elevate the flavor, kept them coming back for more each season. Normally, they watched the Christmas edition as well; but last year was kind of a mess without trying to fit in one more thing. December had certainly been a hectic month, and the old year was best to be left in the past.

"Is it back on yet?" Yasmin shouted from the other side of the closed bathroom door. "I'm almost out." She hollered over the sound of the water running into the sink.

"Take your time, Yas! You're good." Cybil bolted over to where the remote was sitting on their refurbished coffee table, also known as the foot rest. Quickly snatching up the small black rectangle, she tapped on the mute button to silence the man talking about real-estate values going up in their area. He was a new businessman in town, named Stew Duringo, with a cheesy sounding voice and a mannerism that naturally crawled under people's skin.

From the outside, his appearance would have someone believing that he was a wealthy man in charge of a Fortune 500 company. But reality was a bit different. No one liked him, according to what Cybil had overhead while working at Mark's Crafts and Art Supplies, and she couldn't understand what he saw in the empty old office building along Main Street. Speculations ranged from him transforming it into a tanning salon, from seeing fake tan lines under his shirt collars, to others claiming that he was going to open up a goat yoga space with a fad drink café. Then there were those who said he was actually in town to take over the art gallery that Christine Heighner was in the process of selling. Either way, all of the rumors were apparently wrong, as the man proclaimed the launch of his own real-estate business on their television screen.

"Wow." Yas strolled out, watching the ad in relief that she hadn't missed anything. "He must have a chunk of change to be advertising on the local stations already. I mean, he hasn't even opened his doors yet, and is getting the word out on his business."

"Well, that just means that he knows what he's doing when it comes to marketing." Cybil glanced up at the jumping bunny mascot beside Mr. Duringo and took note of the digitally added background of a farm when his logo appeared. "Or at least an idea of what to do."

Thirty agonizing seconds later, Yas and Cybil were excited to finally return to the show they had been watching. After a panel of three judges deliberated, and the host dragged out the results with regurgitated information of what already happened, the two friends celebrated Sydney Dashimon's win. When the cameras panned to the saddened faces of the contestants who lost, both women shook their heads and pointed at the man who chose to bake a brownie.

"Do you think that the bakers they pick for the show have ever watched one of these episodes before?"

Yas cleaned up her end of the couch, and looked over at her roommate in thought. "I believe the baker with the purple hair…who got eliminated in the second week…I think she was the one who said she loved watching the show, and that it was a dream come true to be invited this season."

"Yeah, but they can say anything they want."

"True." Yas brushed her curly hair away from her eyes as she went about starting to do the dishes. The dishwasher was having issues again, and with their landlord on vacation in Colorado, they didn't wish to bother her until she came home.

Sylvia Johnson was a wonderful lady, who owned a semi-large estate that had been passed down through the family for generations. At one point, the Johnson's property had covered a vast six hundred acres of cultivated ground and forest lands. However, around the time of the Great Depression, one of her ancestors made some poor investments and it hadn't been the same since. Her father, Issac Johnson, donated a substantial amount to extend the nearby state park a year before he passed, leaving his daughter with two hundred acres and their surname engraved in a memorial stone for all to read. Though its former glory would never be fully restored, with Sylvia's hands on the reins, the place was thriving and was back on its feet in no time.

"Did you see that a new donut shop is going in near the highway ramp?" Cybil munched down on the last remnants of her snack.

"Yep. I wonder what Regina's father, the Donut King, is going to do about it." Yas smirked into the soapy water where her hands were scrubbing away at one of their pots. "Ralph says that he ran into him at the post office yesterday, and said you could literally see the blood vessels about to pop on his temples."

"I can't believe that the plans were even approved at the township meeting, considering who's on the board." Cybil pulled the filled trash bag from the can and collected the recyclables from a smaller bin by the sink.

"Well, my sources say that although his cousin still sits on the council, there has been bad blood between those two for a few months now."

"Sources? What sources?"

"I don't reveal where I get my information."

Cybil chuckled at the notion as she tied the trash bag closed; remembering only afterwards that she forgot to put the empty fish food container inside. "You don't work for a paper, and you're not a freelance journalist. So spill!"

"Fine. JuJu Lee." Yas watched her friend burst out in laughter.

"JuJu Lee? The one who runs the noodle shop out near the new workout gym?" Cybil couldn't believe her ears. "She's battier than a fruit fly, you know that."

"I admit that she's a bit odd. But that doesn't mean that *everything* she says is farfetched. Remember when she predicted that the high school football team would make it to the state championship? She was right then." Yas defended.

"True. But to quote a movie I once saw: 'Even a stopped

clock is right two times a day.'"

Cybil's roommate nodded. "Okay, okay. Still, you didn't see her when she told me that. I mean, the look in her eyes was way more serious than I've ever witnessed before. She came into Ralph's last night and…" Yas leaned in as though she was afraid the walls had ears. "JuJu even told me that she feared one of them was going to die within a fortnight."

About the Author:

Sarah Ickes has her Associates Degree in Art and Design. She has always held a passion for writing since her first publication of a poem in fifth grade. Not only does she pursue writing, but she also creates artwork that is available for purchasing; such as the illustrations and book cover of this novel. History is of a special interest to her, as she enjoys learning about the past. Please visit her website for more details or follow her on social media.

www.SarahIckesArt.com

Thank you for reading my book, and I hope
you enjoyed it!

www.ingramcontent.com/pod-product-compliance
Lightning Source LLC
Chambersburg PA
CBHW020610160726
47991CB00002BA/716